‹ GOLD ›

‹GOLD›

GERALDINE MILLS

Little
Island

Galyon

Eastern Beach

Lupus Point

N
W   E
S

Serpens

Isleta Point

Vasuri

Rocky Beach

Colmen Pier

Mannioc

Colmen

In the w ds ar rames of gol
A jo   to behold,
ly tr ated with the ca deserved
Will save ou dy orld.

GOLD

First published in 2016 by
Little Island Books
7 Kenilworth Park
Dublin 6W
Ireland

ISBN: 978-1-910411-55-1

A British Library Cataloguing in Publication record for this book is available from the British Library.

Insides designed and typeset by redrattledesign.com
Cover design by Lauren O'Neill

Printed in Poland by Drukarnia Skleniarz

Little Island receives financial assistance from
The Arts Council/An Chomhairle Ealaíon and the Arts Council of Northern Ireland

10 9 8 7 6 5 4 3 2 1

Watch them closely and they will teach you the way.
If you listen to them carefully you can recognise their needs from the sounds they make. Agitated or content. There will be days when they need to be cooled down.
Days when they have to huddle around one another to keep warm.
In the dark they are the life of it all.

from *The Book of Gold*

To Lia Rose and all her cousins

PART I

Orchard

CHAPTER 1

Father steadies me while I step into the white protective suit. It's so big for me it's like I'm being swallowed in a gulp by one of those huge gigantiums that are in our Cosmology game. I roll up the sleeves and the trouser cuffs so that I won't be engulfed altogether, then zip myself up. The hood scritch-scratches the side of my face as I tuck my hair in around each side of it before tightening the toggles. That's enough to get the wobblies doing somersaults in my belly. Father calls them butterflies, but I've never seen an insect of any kind, let alone know what it feels like to have them inside me. Esper would call me a dizzard if I told him. The Sagittars have warned us not to waste energy on feelings, so I keep very quiet.

Before I know it, my brother is zipped up too and we're ready to go.

'These are my sons, Starn and Esper,' Father says to the workers who are filing into the pollination station, pulling on their suits, just like us. I'm happy that Father introduces me first. My brother isn't. He scowls at me. Twins are like that. One always wanting to be first in the line: to get the food, to get the smile, to be praised. I watch the workers scan their Sigma-cards before there is the scrinch of the big metal gates opening. One by one, they trundle through to the three interlocking domes of the triome.

Father still calls it a coaxiorum day, just like he did when we were smaller. That's what he always calls something real nice, something that doesn't happen very often. Sometimes it's a piece of malt stick that he has been able to barter from the Stores or an outing to Biblion, even a game of gazillony. The pollination station is another big event. Because the pollination season is nearly at its end, he wants to show us how it's done. He would really like us to graduate as pollinators when we leave Academy. 'It's the most important job you can do,' he says. 'It's the only way we can survive.'

I don't want to be a pollinator. But I can't tell him that.

Father checks us over to make sure that we are in order. He swipes his Sigma-card and the big gates open, this time for us. Then we walk with him into the enclosed space of the station. Even though he has told us all about it, day in day out, it's like nothing I have ever seen. The pictures on my E-pistle haven't prepared me one little bit.

Huge lights shine from every section of the triome, making it as bright as sunlight. It's almost too much for my eyes and I have to shield them as it beams down along row after row of trees.

'It's all a funny pink colour,' I say, straining my neck to look around me. The pink is everywhere in the three domes that protect the whole area of trees from the choking ash that hangs in the grey world outside. It's as if we were enveloped in a big bright-pink cloud.

'That's the colour of the apple blossom, oh-son-of-mine,' he says.

'Alpha,' my brother and I say in unison.

Our heads turn in every direction to see apple trees growing in straight lines as far as the eye can see. Lift-baskets are parked beside each tree and already pollinators are standing in the lifts that move up along the branches. They take the pollen from one flower on one tree and move to the next, brushing the minuscule grains into the centre of the petals so that the flower will be fertilised.

Then there will be fruit.

'Busy as little bees,' Father says, waving his hand all around him in a great sweep.

The more people that become pollinators the more fruit there will be. The more trees that the workers pollinate the more rations they can get at the end of the week. We hope that if the fruit ripens then Father will be able to bring home an apple for us to taste again this year. Because he was Premium Worker of Orchard Territory for the last three years, he was given an apple for each of us at harvest time. I can still taste it, its scent, its shiny red skin. And, oh, its sweet crunch as I sank my teeth into it. I just held the flesh there in my mouth and let the sugars dance all over my tongue. It was the best thing that had happened to us in a long time.

Each year, everyone is frightened that some catastrophe

will befall us again and there will be no fruit. When we were very little, the Interim Winds came unexpectedly just after pollination. The flowers were blown away and there was no fruit at all. We were too small to remember it, but when Father talks about it, he calls it the Black Year. The Sagittars built the poly-cover domes after that to make sure it never happens again.

Father says it was the smartest thing our rulers ever did. Normally they are so busy fighting among themselves or making up silly rules just to make our lives harder that nothing gets done. Father says that they don't know their tail-bones from their funny-bones. He thinks we need new people to guide us out of this dark age but no-one has the courage to fight the Sagittars. He says they are a catastrophe.

We watch, mesmerised, as the lift-baskets go up and down, the workers move around the tree, pollen wands swishing all over the place. A man in a white suit and with a badge on his hat comes over to us. He has red, roundy cheeks just like the apples they are trying to make.

'Would you like to have a go?' he says to us.

We both look at Father.

'If you think it's OK?' he says, turning to the man and then back to us.

Appleface nods, waves his hand across to where the lift-baskets come down to ground level. We wait until there is one available. Then all three of us step in and close the support belts around us. Father presses the starter control and it swings us up into the air.

CHAPTER 2

U p, up, up we go. It is only when we are at eye level with the branch covered in the palest of blossoms that he stops it.

'You'll learn all about this in Senior Academy,' he says, 'but there's nothing like a head start.'

He shows us how to take the wand and brush it off the part of the flower called the anther that holds the pollen. Then he touches the pollen onto another part called the stigma and the tiny grains move down the tube called the style into the ovary where the fruit then starts to grow.

'That's all it takes to make an apple,' he tells us. 'Want to try?'

'Please,' Esper cries in excitement as he takes the wand, but I'm not that impressed. I try to hide my disappointment. I'm looking really hard but if there's an apple forming on the twig then I'm not seeing it. Nothing. Nada. I was so sure the fruit would grow straight away once the pollen tipped off the stigma.

Esper will just call me a dizzard again so I keep my mouth shut as he paints one flower with the tiny grains and then the next. I'm much more interested in the way the lift-basket moves up and down, taking workers from the ground to the air in seconds and then back down again. Everywhere I look there are wands swishing this way and that like music playing way down low. We are as close as we can go to the roof of the triome. Outside is the dirty sky.

'Starn, it's your turn,' Father says.

I'm nervous as I stretch out my left hand to take the wand from my brother, afraid I'll be clumsy and mess the whole thing up.

'You know by now not to use that hand.'

I quickly put my left hand behind my back and take the wand in my right, hoping no-one else has seen, or I will be in trouble. The Sagittars say the left hand is bad.

'Tell me again, Father, how it works,' I say, as I brush the wand in the way I saw Esper do. 'Where does the pollen go then?'

But Esper is there before him.

'Down the style into the ovary,' he tells me and anyone else within earshot. 'You'd have to be a dizzard not to know that. Being a pollinator is the coolest job.'

That's my bro: full of knowledge and wants everyone to know it.

I say nothing. Of course the bees did a much better job of it. They knew which flowers were ready to be pollinated and which ones weren't. That's why they produced so much more fruit than wand-swishing pollinators. They'll never, ever be as good as bees. I want to shout this out to my brother, but I keep the words hidden in my cheeks.

I hand the wand back to Esper. Father lets me work the

lever to move the lift-basket and that's the best thing ever. I move it across and up and down. The basket follows my instructions and takes us where I say. I am really good at this, up above the ground pretending I am in an aeroplane. Just when I'm really getting the hang of it, I shift the lever too quickly and Esper is jerked away from his task. The wand falls out of his hand. We watch it dive

down

down

down

through the lift to the ground below. Catastrophe. All that precious pollen lost!

Father grabs the lever from me. 'I can't bring you anywhere.' Then he shifts the gear again and the lift-basket begins to move down the length of the tree until we hit ground level. But I know what he's thinking: *Why can't you be like your brother? If I knew you were going to act like a baby then I would have left you at home.*

I am so embarrassed I just want to scurry away and hide. The siren goes off and wobblies start in my stomach again. Does everyone know what I did?

'That's not fair.' Esper glares at me.

I miss Mother.

When we get to the bottom, Appleface is standing there with the wand in his hand. He calls Father into the office. Esper and I shuffle against the wall. My skin is shaking. I don't know what's keeping them. The pollination station sucks.

'Time to go,' Father says when he finally comes back to us.

I am so relieved, I go towards him but he pushes me away. Guess we've lost our chance of an apple this apple-time.

He puts his hands on our shoulders and steers us towards the Defender of the Seed. We stand in the white, white room while a small man with every part of him covered except for his eyes takes a tiny vacufill and runs it all across our suits. The machine beeps each time it locates a grain of pollen and it's sucked into the clear sac that is attached to the end of the machine.

I cannot see anything happening, the grains are so tiny. By the time they are finished with us, a little speck of yellow is at the end of the sac. I want to know why.

'Gathering any pollen grains that have escaped, then sending them back to Labspace. They'll experiment to see if they can tell which flowers are ready to accept the pollen and which are not. Then they'll get onto the plant nursery to see if they can get new species to grow. So there will be better crops, just like the bees could do.'

Told you! I say under my breath.

'Mind yourselves on the way home,' Father says as he walks us to the gate and we head towards the pedal-pod station. The platform is packed with workers who have just finished the early shift. Father has to stay longer today to take stock of how many trees are left to receive the pollen. I think of the pollen grains I lost on the fallen wand. All those apples!

The almond trees were the first plants to go. Then corn, then soya. The bees were exhausted, being driven around the world to pollinate all those trees and plants. When the ash came it choked any blossoms that hadn't been blown off by the Interim Winds. There wasn't enough nectar for the bees and they got so weak they just died away. We have einkorn for our breakfast and our bread because the wind pollinates that grain.

But so many other things are gone from us. Father gets all excited talking about raspberries and blueberries, pears and plums. Mother used to tell us too about picking blackberries and making something called jam. We can only imagine what they tasted like.

We await our turn before we pile into the carriages. I get all wobbly inside until I am safely pedalling away. Last time we were on the pedal-pod there was a commotion at the other end of the platform. We saw four helmets with spears on top push their way through the crowd. The Sagittars. They grabbed a man by his raggy coat and pulled him away. An indigent who had been caught trying to sleep behind one of the shelters. Indigents are homeless, having lost their homes when the ash fell. Lots of them have died but the Sagittars are trying to clear the territory of any of them still left. If they find them in open spaces they gather them up and lock them away in the detention unit. We nearly lost Father once when he stepped in to protect an old man from having his hand twisted behind his back by them as they carted him away. They warned Father that he was treading on thin ice. Father laughed it off but he has to be careful.

Soon we're in our seats, pedalling along, leaving the pollination station well behind us; hoping that apples will form. That the outer part will flesh out and the inner part will create new seeds that can all go into the seed bank. Everyone looks to the air in hope that there will be a summer. That the wind will blow the clouds from the sun just long enough to give the trees the natural light they need to fill out for a good harvest.

We pedal out through the plains of dust and scrub, away past the big umbrella leaves of the gunnera that bear down on us from every side. It's one of the few plants that have survived the ash and continue to grow all year. Their seeds float down the waterways and they plant themselves in different spots. They are as big as trees now and if it wasn't for them we would have no oxygen to breathe. The Sagittars have decreed that no-one goes near the big floppy leaves, as they keep us alive. They're left to grow away all around us on their own.

I shiver as we pass the isolation unit in the distance. Beside that is the plant nursery where they're trying to get new plants to grow in the poor light. Beyond that: Virus Islands. Five of them altogether, forbidden islands, the ones the Sagittars say are full of viruses like the one that killed Mother and Seelah. They are out of bounds, so that no more disease is brought back to Orchard Territory. It would be a brave person who would take a chance trying to cross the strait, which is teeming with zanderhag fish. They would be devoured in an instant.

Sometimes a swirl of ash might clear like a curtain

opening in the world. We catch a glimpse of the islands' humped backs rising out of the sea. But as soon as it clears it closes in again and it's as if they're not there at all. It was where Father and Mother grew up before they came to the Territories, BA – Before the Ash.

'I'm definitely going to be a pollinator when I leave Academy,' says Esper. 'Guess you blew your chances.'

'Shut –' But I stop myself. I'm in enough trouble already. I hate him when he's like this, going on and on about all he knows and what he's going to do. The things I hate, he loves. The things I love, he hates. His hair is brown, mine fair. He loves things of the earth; for me it's the sky.

'As different as winter and summer,' Mother used to call us.

Before we know it, pollination will be over and winter will be upon us. Father hopes he will get work again in the energy centre, harvesting as much wind as possible to keep everything moving, enough heat for all the dark days. If he works really hard we will have privileges: like using our E-pistles for twice as long. Last year he didn't know whether he was going to have work or not until that morning when the message came through in his cloud-box. He worries all the time about it.

We let ourselves into the apartment. It's very quiet. Just the two of us moving around in the semi-darkness. There are jobs we must do before we prepare for sleep. Tidy up the gel-bags, put our E-pistles in the docking station. Get the orgone water ready for the morning. I put the beads in the flask that sits on the food station overnight. Then cover them with water from the tap. When we wake up the water will be safe to drink with all the minerals that will keep our blood alkaline so we can stay healthy.

The light begins to fade. Soon the hall will be covered in darkness; the hall where Father's room is and the door opposite it. The door that is always closed, the door to the room where Mother and Seelah died. The room we're no longer allowed into. It will be bivi-bag hour by the time Father gets home.

CHAPTER 3

'Uppity up, Starn,' Father calls out in his happy, happy morning voice, 'Uppity up. Esper'll have all the vita-shake gobbled up on you if you don't get those limbs out of your bivi-bag.'

He comes in, all smiley-eyed and swishy-tailed, talking to me as if I was a baby. He seems to forget what age I am. He flicks the switch in his hand and the blinds of my bedroom window spring open. I can feel the dark of winter straight away and drag my bivi-bag over my head.

'Vita-shakes suck, winter sucks,' I say to him as he pulls the covers from me and I lie there shivering.

'Now, Starn, cut out that nonsense. You know this weather is going to be with us for the next few months; you might as well get used to it. So stop whinge-gaggling. It's not that bad; you get to stay indoors and read your E-pistle and that's better than shovelling grime from the tracks of the pedal-pod, now isn't it?'

I can't argue with that. One of the worst things we have to do is to take our scrape-blades and shovel the ash and grime that falls down from the sky when the Interim Winds come. It gets through our masks and leaves us all coughing and spluttering. Sometimes Esper can't breathe and he has to be put in a breathing lung until he can do so himself again.

'Do you know how lucky you are?' Father starts. 'I remember …' and I shut off my ears and start humming a tune before he starts on his list of how hard life was for him just after the ash fell.

I'm sitting up in bed at this stage and he's fracking on to the cold air, ding dong, blah de blah. All about the lists of stories that he read as a boy that he's going to cloud-grab for me and my brother. Then he starts on about what it was like having books made of paper. Not like the E-pistles that Esper and I now read. I drop myself out of my bivi-bag. Brrr, it's freezing. I pull on my day suit as fast as I can and slide out the door of my room and across the floor to the food station.

Just as Father said, Esper is there finishing his shake. He never seems to mind when the temperature drops and it's too cold to do anything, indoors or out.

'Finally, oh-son-of-mine,' Father says and picks up the vita-shake. 'Come on, slide it down the little red lane. And I don't want to see a Tartesah nose.' I hate when he refers to my nose, which is supposed to be like our great-aunt's. It turns up a little but he says it turns up even more when I don't like something. He laughs but I don't see the funny side.

'Father, I'm not a baby.'

'Well, don't act like one, then,' Esper says.

'Shut up.' On days like this my brother sucks.

'How often have I told you, you only have one another –'

'So we have to be good to one another,' we both chorus. It makes us laugh. For a nano-second I don't hate Esper.

'Give me the right hand this time. Now drink up or you know there will …'

I hide my left hand behind my back and let the drink slide down the little red lane without it hitting my taste-buds. But each time it gets me, the slimy gunk. Yuck!

'Don't do that,' Father says when I wipe my mouth with the back of my hand. 'Anyone would think you were being brought up by indigents.'

A shivery feeling creeps down my back. Just the mention of them and I think back to the man at the station.

I have a big drink of orgone water to wash it all down. The pot of einkorn bubbles away on the heat ring. He fills three bowls full of the steaming porridge and we sit and eat. When we're finished, Father brings us over to the measure-gauge and checks if we have put on a stretch. We have both grown a millimetre, which is funny because Esper drinks a lot more vita-shakes than me.

'See, Father, I grow whether I drink my shake or not.'

'You know I have to fill in the report and if either of you is not growing then I'm in big trouble with the Sagittars.'

'Can we play gazillony in the park today?' Esper pipes up.

Usually Father lets him do whatever he wants. He always gets his own way. But I love gazillony too, so I wouldn't mind going out. I love it best when we skim the hubcaps across the court and get them in the box.

'Not today,' Father says. 'I have to go to work.'

'But you said –'

'No buts, there was a message in my cloud-box last night. All workers have to go in today. There's an emergency.'

'There's always an emergency,' I mumble.

I shouldn't have said that. He's back at me straight away.

'I thought you were old enough to understand by now that when work comes I have to grab it. And what would you do without the special privileges you get when I do extra? You'll be allowed to use your E-pistle for the next two weeks without rationing. I bet lots of your friends wished their father worked emergency. You wouldn't get them complaining like you.'

I know. But it means he will be out all day and we'll be on our own. That's OK for the first hour or two but then it gets so boring because we can't leave the room for more than twelve minutes or Child Watch Central will set off the alarm. That's how he checks us out – on the CWC cameras in the living room. It's the Sagittars' way of ensuring workers are not caught up at home when they are needed in the energy centres. We tell him we're too old for that now but he's having none of it.

'Are you going to grab any new stories today? When I was your age, my favourites –'

'We know,' we both groan together. 'But we don't have books now.'

'Oh, OK, so.' He laughs as he picks up his pedal-pod helmet. 'Make sure you're near the CWC camera when I tune in,' he tells us. 'How can Child Watch Central tell me you're OK if you're not in its sight? There was a delay on Friday and I couldn't locate you. That really scared me! You must never do that again. You know how much it worries me. Promise me.'

We promise. Then he clicks the remote and he's out the door and onto the lift that will bring him down to the ground and the pod station.

CHAPTER 4

The door has barely closed when Esper grabs his E-pistle. I sit on my gel-bag trying to decide what to do. I could draw with my stylus or play with my collection of bodsticks or … or … Already I'm bored. There's diddly squat adventure around here.

We can't go outside without Father, and anyway, it's too cold and our fingers will be frozen in the time a Sagittar can say *psittacosis*. Some days there isn't enough heat to keep us warm and we have to climb into our bivi-bags. Even though I hate it, Father is right. If he doesn't do the overtime we'll end up on the streets like the indigents with no place to go. And we do have the extra ration of energy he will get for our E-pistles. Which is better than the slap of a wet gunnera leaf any day.

'Hey, Starno, what are you going to grab?' Esper slouches on his gel-bag and starts scrolling.

'Don't call me Starno.'

'Starno. Starno. Starno. Get over it.'

I grab my stuff-sack and fling it at him. It gets him right where I wanted to. He falls off his seat and his E-pistle thuds to the floor.

'If you've broken it you're in big trouble.'

'Well, Espo Espo Espo, that'll teach you not to call me names again.'

He picks up his E-pistle and presses the check button. 'You're very lucky, it still works.' He puts up his hand to say we're quits.

'So! What now?'

'I'm going for the one I grabbed last time. About lost animals.'

That's my brother. Everything he reads is about animals. Ones that lived a long, long time ago and others that lived just before the Ash. When he was very small he would pretend he was something called a badger and make a burrow for himself in his bivi-bag. Mother used to say that if he had a choice he would prefer to be a badger instead of a boy.

I think she was right.

'Again? You always go for the same thing.'

'So what? You're as bad,' he challenges me. 'Bet you're going to get something on aeroplanes.'

There's no denying that I love to read about the way people travelled before pedal-pods, when there was lots of fuel and people flew across the world. I hope Scroll-box has something new on that today.

Esper wanders over to the docking station by the door and plugs in his E-pistle. He speaks into the microphone. 'I want a story about pangolins.'

Ping and the story appears on his screen.

'Pangolins. I bet there was no such thing. You're just making it up to show off.'

'Look here, farty pants. See! That's what they looked like.'

On his screen is a strange creature with a coat of brown horny scales like metal armour. It used its long narrow snout and sticky rope-like tongue to poke down ant hills and suck up all the little insects. They had no teeth, though, so they couldn't chew things. That's what the Sagittars say will happen to us if we don't eat our greens.

Changing my mind about aeroplanes, I go over to the docking station. 'A story about birds,' I command. *Ping*, and there it is on the screen, waiting for me to devour it.

'You tell me now. What's so special about birds?' Esper asks.

'You know!'

'Wings, able to fly. No pedal-pods?'

'You got it. If the trees hadn't been destroyed, well …' I say.

My story unfolds on the screen. The ones that really interest me are kites. Like other birds of prey, they followed the wind. They beat their wings very little, and when the wind was very high they stayed up there with it. But if it was low then they stayed low too. I'd love to be a bird. To be up above the buildings and able to look down on the triome, the goober farms, the energy centre. I'd be really happy to see a bird. Any bird.

The CWC alarm fills the room with its noise.

'Greens time,' says the machine.

'Yuck! I hate greens.'

'We had better eat them,' says Esper, 'or we might get sick again.'

We go over to the growth chamber, a glass tank filled with arcillite. It's packed with nutrients and doesn't need water, as other plants do. Because they can't grow outside, every apartment has to grow them indoors. We eat them, even though we hate them.

Afterwards I down-scroll stuff about volcanoes. I read that the exact number of volcanoes is unknown. There were things called 'volcanic fields' that had a load of eruption centres. That's what happened: when the sea floor shifted, Stromboli, Trakula Ruapehu, Melimoo, Turrialba and hundreds more coughed up all their lava and dirt right on top of us.

The E-pistle is just going to tell me about conder cones, maars and shield volcanoes when Esper shouts across at me: 'Let's play gauntlets. We haven't played it for ages.'

'Naw!'

'You just don't want to play because you lost so badly last time.'

'Not. It's sooo boring,' I reply.

But he's right. I did lose badly. Gauntlets is a dare game. We made it up after we did a project in Academy about the knights of old who used to throw down their big gloves of armour to challenge their enemies. The time he's talking about is when he threw down the gauntlet and dared me to drink a whole vita-shake without stopping for breath. He knew I'd gag. I couldn't do it. I'd promised myself that if I ever got the chance again, but …

'Can't you see I'm reading?' I say defensively. 'Just cos you're bored doesn't mean I have to drop what I'm doing.'

'Chicken-face, chicken-face. You can't bear the fact that I'll trounce you as always.'

'Not so. I just want to read about this –'

But before I can open my mouth he's run down the hall and into the laundro to fetch the big glove that Father used to use in the energy centre when he had to carry hot panels for one of the compressors, until holes burnt through it and it was no good for that any more. Which is how we came to have it at home.

'Here, you can start.'

It's so big, when I pull it on it goes way beyond my elbow. Hmmm, now, what could be a good dare for my brother? It's not as if there are a lot of things to do in our little apartment.

When we've played it before, most of them haven't been real dares at all, just silly things like posting remarks about Sagittars on our pages or making faces out the window at anyone passing so I really have to try and get him back with a good one. I pull off the glove and throw it down in front of him.

'I dare you to run down the stairs – blindfolded and without your thermo-suit – out onto the street and back again.'

Apart from the fact that it's freezing out there, it's been drummed into us from the time we were allowed to stay at home that we're not supposed to open our door for any reason when Father's away and that's the rule.

'Easy-peasy,' Esper says, without a bother, slipping his hand into the glove. I find an old cloth in the laundro basket and tie it around his eyes, blinding him. Then, standing at the door to make sure he doesn't take the blindfold off, I watch him take the stairs, slowly at first until he finds his footing, and soon make it to the bottom. The utility gate opens onto the street and I count to ten before I hear him close it. Then he turns and comes back again. He stumbles just before the top step but makes it, pulls off his blindfold and stands there, shivering. His cheeks are red with the cold and he swings his arms up and down in an effort to get the feeling back into them.

'You'll have to do better than that.' He pulls off the glove and in turn throws it at me. 'Dare you to drink yesterday's leftover vita-shake all in one go.'

So he's going for the same dare again. The smell of it alone after it has been left for a day is like the worst smell ever. But I promised myself back then that I wouldn't let him get me a second time.

I pick up the glove. Then into the kitchen and take out the container with the greeny-brown sludge. I hold my nose as I lift it up. Yuck, yuck, yuck and yuck again. It's worse than smelly gunnera, more like an indigent rotting in the pits. I pinch my nose until it hurts and almost without breathing I chug it down. *Glug glug.*

I hold my lips tight so it doesn't come back up again,

and it slurps its way into my stomach. I want to get sick, but I don't.

'Hah!' I say, when I can safely breathe once more, and throw the glove right back at him. 'I dare you put your gel-bag in front of the CWC screen and block it.'

I see the fear flicker across his eyes: 'But, but … If that goes to Child Watch Central …'

'Chicken-face.'

'… they'll be on top of us all day checking us out.'

'Chicken-face, chicken-face.'

'We won't be able to move.'

I'm jumping up and down inside, thinking I've got him on this one. But some part of him forgets about the fear and he picks up the bag and pushes it right in front of the screen. As soon as the screen is touched the alarm goes off. It screeches all over the room ERROR REPORTED, ERROR REPORTED and just before the third error message comes, which will send a report to the emergency log, he pulls the bag away.

Silence.

'Hah, to you, too,' he says. 'Thought I wouldn't do it, didn't you?'

He's all smug now and works his way around the room, thinking, the gloved hand outstretched, stroking his chin with the other like some ancient scientist about to reveal a great solution to an unfathomable problem.

Then he starts smirking. I hate when he does that. I know, just know, he's going to sting me.

'I am so clever, clever, clever,' he starts, singing and

jumping around like a mallamuck. 'Guess who's going to be the winner again this time.'

There's nothing worse than my brother telling me that before I even know what the challenge is. But I've seen that look before. When he comes up with them he really comes up with them. He walks over to me, slaps the ground. There is the sound of one glove falling.

'The room,' he says.

'What?' My heart falls into a dark place.

'Go into the room.'

'But you know that's forbidden.'

'Go into the room, chicken-face.' He smirks.

'But I've no code.'

'Get it.'

'How?'

'From Father's Visage.'

It's not really Father's. The Visage belongs to the Sagittars for storing different work data. It's a pretty big deal that Father is allowed to bring it home sometimes. And we are not allowed to touch it.

CHAPTER 5

Esper's words do backflips all around my head. What he's asking is the impossible.

'Have you had a memory lapse or something? I can't go in there. You know the rules, and anyway Father trusts us not to.'

'That's no excuse. Chicken-face, chicken-face. I win. Again.'

As if that's not bad enough, the glove sits at my feet, taunting me as well. But how can I go back into that room after what happened there?

We all caught the same psittacosis virus. The Sagittars kept us in isolation for weeks until the blisters, which looked like tiny white flowers, began to dry up. As we got stronger our little sister got weaker. She died in Mother's arms and that was the last we saw of her. Her body was taken away immediately so that no-one else would be infected. But it was too late. Because Mother had stayed home to nurse Seelah while Father was at the energy centre and we were at Academy, she started to get sick again.

A second eruption of blisters meant the worst. The Sagittars ordered Father to shift her to the isolation unit with all the other people who were infected. But he wouldn't budge. He didn't want Mother to move from the place she loved or be separated from us. The Sagittars stopped one week's rations because of it. Mother cried out towards the end, asking Father for some marzipan, which we had never heard of, and some pineapple to quench her thirst, though there hadn't been such fruit since we were born. We had to keep giving her sips of electro-fluid to try and rehydrate her. After that, the room where they died was locked up and we were never allowed into it again.

We know Father goes into the room, but only when he thinks we're asleep. I often see him out of the corner of my eye after he has said goodnight to us. I imagine him as he carries his burdened shoulders down the hall, hear him punch in the code and go in. I lie awake listening to him quietly sobbing. That's why he's insistent that we take our vita-shakes. The Sagittars said that Seelah didn't have enough nutrients in her body to withstand the infection. The same with Mother.

After all that, Esper now wants me to go in there.

'Chicken-face!'

Father always tells us we have choices. Even in the worst situations we can choose to fight or choose defeat. So I could give my brother a good trouncing but that won't be the end of it. He'll never let me forget that I've failed.

There's humongous satisfaction watching his face fall when I turn to him. 'You'll eat those words.'

Grabbing the gauntlet, I tear off down the hall to Father's door, Esper hot on my heels shouting, 'You're wasting your time, you'll never do it.'

I turn the handle and step into Father's room. I haven't really been in here since I had that bad fever and he didn't want me to be out of his sight so he made me sleep in his bivi with a cold cloth on my forehead for two nights, but that was yonks ago.

The Visage is on the shelf by his bivi, his home clothes folded neatly at the end of it. The room seems very empty without him, even though I know he's not too far away. My brother's face is the colour of thunder. 'Father will malafooster you if he catches you.'

'But he won't catch me because you are going to keep an ear out for Child Watch. Remember, if the camera clicks in and we're not in front of it, we're Sagittar fodder. That's not just me, you know. It's the two of us. Getting a little bit nervous now, are you?'

YES. This really flicks his nose out of joint.

I pick up the Visage and switch it on. The first thing I see on the screen is a picture of my brother and me. Father says we are always on his mind and we're never to forget that, no matter what.

I sit on the bivi and start to scroll through his list of files. There are so many of them, and the code could be secreted anywhere. Esper slouches at the door glaring at me, wishing me defeat.

'You're wasting your time,' he says again.

'Well, that's for you to say and me to believe, which I

don't, so give it a break.' I check the dates on the files and most of them haven't been updated for six months. I know he has to change the code every month. It's the law. That makes it a tiny bit easier, because that's what I need to look for: a file updated in the last month.

Most of the remaining files are to do with his timetables for work, like when pollination finishes or when energy centre starts. There's names of the people he works with. But there's nothing here that half resembles a code. Next I go into his Sagittar registration files but there doesn't seem to be anything there either. It could be staring me in the face in some kind of camouflage and I'd be none the wiser.

Now here's something. This might be what I'm looking for. Naw, it's just a list for Opson Stores, recipes for vita-shakes. How to clean out the arcillite tank. Other than home jobs, nothing. Nada.

'Maybe he just keeps it in his head,' I say.

'Well then you're a loser, aren't you?'

'It's not over till it's over.'

The more I search the more I'm being hooked in, all line and sinker. What if I *could* get into the room?

'You're only – quick!' says Esper. 'I can hear the camera logging in. Fast.'

I push the Visage under the bivi-base and dash back to the room just in time for the CWC to send its update. Just being so close to the room has brought up those feelings that were all tucked away inside some little corner of me and now they have come bubbling up. By the time the camera zooms in on us, we're sitting with our E-pistles as if we hadn't moved all day. We stare up as the camera looks into our eyes and takes our photo.

Then Father comes on to say he's on his way home. That puts an end to my search for now. By the time he comes through the door, later that afternoon, it's as if nothing has happened.

'Did you have a good day? Much going on?' says Father.

'Boring,' we both call out, virtually at the same time.

'What are you doing with that old glove?'

'Just playing knights.'

'Glad to see you haven't forgotten the old games.' He laughs and leaves his stuff-sack on the counter.

Later, Esper and I lie in our bivi-bags. All light has gone from the house except for the emergency flickers that are plugged into the wall in the event of a catastrophe. Father checks on us one last time before he heads down the hall to his bivi.

The room's darker than last night. The only sound is the scritch of the einkorn straw in our bags as we turn into our sleep. But sleep won't come. I have a vision of a big black Sagittar hammering at the window and I shiver. I lie there thinking about peregrine falcons; how they can make great swoops and how their beaks have a tooth on each side. So beautiful. They were the fastest creatures on earth. They could fly as fast as an aeroplane.

The code. There's got to be a way to find it.

'Esper, Esper. Know what? You're not going to beat me this time. I'm going to find it,' I whisper.

But my brother doesn't answer me. I lie there listening to him sleeping, muttering away to whoever or whatever he is dreaming about. He does that a lot. I never know what he's saying. And he never remembers in the morning. Father says it's something to do with all the vita-shakes. But I don't care about that. I can barely wait until daybreak.

CHAPTER 6

ather doesn't have to come in and wake me this morning because I'm up and dressed, blinds open, bivi made. He looks up from the food station.

'Oh-son-of-mine,' he says in his fatherly voice. 'Early to bed and now early to rise, how wise you really are! What has you so smiley-eyed and swishy-tailed?'

'Nothing.'

I look up at him and for a minute he must think I'm Esper because he looks at me that way. Softer, gentler.

Act normal, normal, I tell myself as Esper and I sit down for our shakes. I pull my usual face as I drink down the gunk and wipe my mouth with the back of my hand. I peer over at my twin, trying to make eye signals.

'Going to try it again,' I whisper when father turns his back to stir the einkorn. Esper looks at me as if I've gone doolally. 'I'll do this if it kills me.'

'What are you talking about?'

'The code.'

'It's over, forget it.'

'Well, I'm still playing. Who's chicken-face now? All of a sudden afraid of your own dare. Called your bluff. Ha!'

'We can't go in there,' he says, going paler and paler. 'With or without the code, you know it's out of bounds.'

'You should have thought of that before you threw down the gauntlet to me.'

'What are you two whispering about?'

'Just wondering what time you're going to work today, Father?' I say.

Esper is still slurping his drink. There's a dirty brown rim around his mouth.

'Well, guess what?' Father replies, as he puts our bowls of einkorn in front of us. 'Our team increased the energy output by three yesterday and I just got a message in my cloud-box to say I have earned enough points to take a parental day.'

'Alpha,' my brother says.

I suddenly become very interested in my cereal so that he doesn't see my disappointment. I love my father but this is one time I want him gone.

'What about you, Starn? Is it alpha for you too?'

'Yano,' I blurt. 'I, I …'

'Well, oh-son-of-mine, you're stuck with me today, so you'll have to put up with me. Any ideas what we'll do?'

He ruffles my hair as if I was still a baby. Sometimes he treats us as if we were Seelah's age. It's as if he never wants us to grow up.

'Can't we just stay at home?' I grumble.

'You really are a very contrary boy,' he chides me. 'Don't you realise the great treat it is for me that I don't have to work today and can be with you?'

Before I can open my mouth, Esper chimes in: 'Let's do Biblion.'

Esper says that just to please Father. He knows he loves to go to the book repository more than anywhere else. It was what Mother and he did when they came off the islands and settled here. They worked in what they called libraries back then. Floor to ceiling, big books stuffed with words, others with pictures, drawings. Shelf after shelf of them. They were as important to him as breathing. He loves to talk about their days back then, when their lives were full of books.

'That's more like it,' Father says.

'Biblion sucks,' I say.

'That seems to be the only word you know this weather. Well, if you don't want to go, then' – he takes a big fatherly breath – 'there's always the Nanny Care for you and I can bring just Esper. I don't want a repeat of pollination station.'

I go red inside and out. He knows that's the last thing I want to do, being nannied with the tinies.

'OK, so.'

'Now, we'll hear no more about it. Today is a good day to go because they'll be taking new books out of storage and the light will be just right for the more delicate ones.'

We bundle ourselves into our thermo-suits, pull on our masks and our helmets and head off to the pedal-pod station.

The station is packed. One by one we pile into the four-seater carriages and soon everyone is pedalling furiously on the tracks going to their own places. People get on and off at the different stops. If Father had his way he'd have everyone coming to Biblion. My legs are exhausted and I try to take little breaks, but a woman beside me notices me slacking and shouts in her loudest voice: 'We have a pedal-pooper right here.'

Everyone turns and stares at me. I wish I could be sucked up into the clouds.

Biblion's the last stop on the track and only two other families stay on until then. The cold comes up to meet us as we stand around, waiting for someone to open the door, all of us shuffling our feet to keep warm. Two months' time and it will be too cold for anyone to come out. Sagittars stand at the door and check our passes. The one with the scar down the right side of his face so his eye is partially closed looks Father up and down.

'Hiram Brock?'

'Yes, sir!'

'Your boys?'

'Yes, sir!'

He checks Father's photo-image, then back to his face again before he swipes the pass in his machine and shoves it back into Father's hand.

'Thank you, sir,' Father says politely, as the Defender of the Page opens the door and lets us step into the Origins Room. We all breathe more easily then.

'At least we're not on our own,' Father says as the other families follow in behind us. 'Starn, take that long face off you, or I'll have to bring you to the medics.'

I try to smile. This must be Father's favourite place in all of Orchard. Maybe it's where he feels closest to Mother. But today it's no contest for me. I know just where I want to be.

The main room has cabinets full of old paper and screens telling how the first paper was made, something called papyrus, and machines that printed the first books. It shows trees being pulped and brought to factories and how all the water was squeezed out of them and then dried in big warehouses. That was when there were trees of course. Nearly all the libraries were destroyed by the Ash, millions and millions of books. Father and Mother's library went the same way. Any paper that could be saved was stored in repositories all over the world.

The smaller room holds a selection of books that are kept in a specially controlled atmosphere so that they don't get mouldy or anything. The Defender of the Page turns a new one every day and you can see what's written there. But you can't handle them. No-one is ever allowed to handle them. Last time we came, we saw a book called *Around the World in Eighty Days* which was about a man travelling all over the earth in steamers and trains. Before that we saw a page from a book about banks collapsing. That was so boring.

'Look,' Father says, 'how amazing is that!' His voice rises so that the other people who are coming from the Origins Room turn to see what's going on. He is almost in on top of the glass he's so excited. The Defender of the Page shouts at him to step back, and Father pulls himself away.

'It's da Vinci's notebooks. Leonardo da Vinci's notebooks. Can you believe it, a page from two of them?' He's more animated than I have seen him in a long time.

'It was your mother's dream to see them one day, mine too. I can't believe some of them survived. Boys, now this is what I call alpha.'

He's never used our word before; his excitement is catching. We go as close to the cabinet as we are allowed so we can see what all the fuss is about.

At first all I see is a mish-mash of writing in cursive that makes no sense to me. I'd have just given up if it wasn't for the little drawings up and down the pages. I study them one by one.

'Oh!'

That's all I can say when I see what they are about.

'Esper, do you think they are what I think they are?'

'Are they …?'

'Yes, some kind of flying machine, and there, look – a type of glider.'

'Father, you're right. It is alpha.'

'Imagine hundreds of years ago, before anything took to the sky, other than birds that is, this man was designing machines that could fly. Your mother and I had seen copies of the drawings in books but to see the real thing is just …'

Whatever words he's looking for won't come.

We move along to the second page. This is even more alpha than the other. Down the right-hand side of it are beautiful drawings of birds flying, as if their wings were catching the wind. As if they were keeping themselves up in the sky by moving their wings and tails. Sometimes they even used their wings as brakes. Imagine if I'd missed that!

I stand there staring at them until the Sagittar orders us to move on.

'Can we come back tomorrow? Please, to see what's on the next page when it gets turned?'

'And you were the one who didn't want to come!' Father laughs. 'I wish we could, son, but afraid not. This is a special. It's for one day only. Tomorrow is roll-over time. It will probably be no more exciting than a train timetable. Now let's head home.'

'Thank you, Father,' I say as we go towards the door.

'What's this? Did I get something right for once?'

CHAPTER 7

It's a freezeday, one of those days when the Polar Jet Stream pulls the Arctic air on top of all of us and we know before we put our noses out the door that it will be blistering cold. Frozen spray from the waterways whips up and covers everything: streets, pods, walls. Father is on early shift at the energy centre, so he's here to supervise us before we leave for Academy. He warns us to make sure that we wear our thermo-suits and cover our faces too or our noses will fall off. We laugh but we listen to him all the same. Master says that if the sun dies it will only take eight minutes and twenty seconds for the world to turn to a frozen state.

As we are leaving, Father comes down the hall scratching his head.

'Either of you seen my Visage? I need to collate yesterday's information. I was sure I had it by my bivi.'

'No,' we both say, far too quickly. 'Do you want us to have a look?'

'Would you, please? It can't be very far away.'

I do a really good impression of searching, lifting up gel-bags, looking in drawers, behind CWC, his stuff-sack.

'Could you have left it in the energy centre?' I say.

'Didn't think I did, but you know you may be right. I'll search it out and sign you if I find it. You know, I'd forget my head …'

'… if it wasn't stuck to you,' we both chime back and laugh.

Our lesson pads, our lunch shakes, our E-pistles are all packed into our stuff-sacks and we head down the stairs. The yellow Academy pod pulls up outside our block and we climb in. It's freezing.

'Hi, Craster. Hi, Tuan.'

We work our way down the pod towards our pals. Craster has a big smile on his face. 'Guess what, guys,' he says. 'I got to the next level of Cosmology. And those cuddly bear-like goveys will become raging fireballs and drive the humanoid gigantiums back to Planet Eris.' He's all excited about the virtual game we have been playing for weeks now. He's the most competitive of us all, wants to be ahead all the time, to be the first to find a universe smaller than is observable. I did too at the beginning, but now I've been sidetracked.

My legs begin to warm up as they turn furiously and we pedal away. The pod loops in around the grids and all the buildings are covered in silver-white stalactites. Beyond that I see the sea but the sea doesn't see me, the water dark and murky swirling around the isolation unit. Beyond that again are Virus Islands. Nobody ever goes there. And if they do they can never come back.

We think that's where the Godwin family went. There is no other explanation. They had invented a new fabric made from ardil fibre. It was very special because it was warm in winter and cool in summer. The Sagittars wanted them to make earth-suits with it and gave them a whole moon-time of rations after they showed it to the committee. They kept the Godwins up night and day finishing the suits. Dafod couldn't come to Academy because he had to work with his family. I remember the day he told me that they were going on a journey. He didn't say where but I could guess. That was the last I saw of him. After two months the Sagittars boarded up their apartment and it was never leased to anyone else.

I often wonder about them. Eaten by zanderhags most likely.

The pod comes to a halt outside the revolving doors of Academy and we all file in. We put our frost masks in the cabinets all along the hall. Then we go and sit in our booths in the class, wire up our earphones.

Master gives us a test about the Jet Stream to see if we can remember what he told us last week. He walks around making sure that we are working and not playing games. 'Starn,' he says sharply, 'get to work.' I stop doodling pictures of birds and try to concentrate.

I record all I can onto my E-pistle, how the tectonic plates shifted, setting off a chain reaction. How volcano after volcano erupted, sending fountains of lava, smoke and ash into the atmosphere. How clouds of dust were carried across the earth, covering the sun for years at a time. How many countries were wiped out altogether.

I remember Master saying that if the wind had meandered

in another direction it would have kept the ash away from us. It could also have destroyed us, as the fast-moving air currents moved vertically and horizontally across the world affecting each landmass differently.

Some small islands were protected from the fallout and the inhabitants there were able to live a good life. But not Orchard. It was covered by ash for years and years. Trees and plants were choked. Animals died. Insects and birds had no food. Birds died. There was no nectar for the bees. Bees died. Then Esper and I were born.

'Let me see what you've written, Starn Brock,' Master says, picking up my E-pistle. 'Hmm,' and 'Hmm,' again. 'Up here,' he says, sending me to the top of the room. I didn't think it was bad enough to get me punished.

But no. He gets me to read it out to the class. He is so surprised at the accuracy of what I've written that he gives me a gold star. He makes such a fuss that I just want to run away and hide.

'Not bad,' my brother says.

The rest of the afternoon drags on and on, and when the siren finally goes I am on the yellow pod before a Sagittar can say *psittacosis*.

Father won't be back for hours, so we let ourselves into the apartment. I kick off my snow-boots and pull on my bivi-shoes. He will be really suspicious if his Visage doesn't turn up very soon. He'll have to report it missing, so I can't let it go that far or there'll be trouble. It's now or never. My last chance.

My belly's on the lookout for pindarvite on harran

bread. It's one of my favourites. Spreading it on as thick as the bread will hold I bite into it.

Yum. It's one of Esper's favourites too. We're both licking our fingers when it hits me. Father's favourite. Now, what would that be?

OF COURSE!

'Think I've got it.' Pushing the rest of the bread into my mouth, I zoom down the hall.

'Not that again,' Esper shouts after me in exasperation. 'What's there to see? An empty room where our mother and sister died? Bringing back all our sadness.'

No way is that going to stop me.

'I'm taking the gauntlet back, cancelling the dare,' he shouts even louder. He must be really scared if he's willing to go that far. He knows that's an even greater disgrace than to fail to do a dare, but I'm not letting him do that.

'Please,' he says, very quietly, but I don't hear what else he says. I'm down the hall trying to stay as calm as the dead, but I get in my own way and wobblies are playing gazillony in my belly. I creep along, not making a sound in case the camera picks up my movements. I head into Father's room, scramble under the bivi-base where I've hidden the Visage, switch it on.

Father's favourite? No prizes for guessing. Of course. Books. I scroll down the list of files again and there it is:

LIBRARY.

Clicking on it, there's another list, as long as winter, of all his favourites. In alphabetical order.

Bees and Society

Bible

Crime and Punishment

Dictionary

Fahrenheit 451

Hamlet

and loads more.

Apart from Dictionary and Bible, I've never heard of them and they've never been shown in Biblion. They must be from a way-back time.

He seems to have a system of grading because typed at the beginning of each one he has some figures and numbers. The dictionary and *Fahrenheit 451* get five alphas α α α α α while *Crime and Punishment* gets only three betas β β β. Every one that I check has been graded in this way.

Greek Art β β β

Life on Earth α α α α

Memoir β β β β

Then I see it: *Room.* That's the title. I click on it and it's an actual story. Written about a little boy and his mother who have been kidnapped by an evil man. I check to see how he's graded it but its sequence is completely different, nothing like the others at all: λ 2 Θ 4 ∪ 6 ρ

I look at it again. Could it be? Yes! It has to be.

'Yahoo!'

I grab the Visage, rush across the hall. Punch in the letters and numbers. Turn the handle.

Stupid me! Must be too excited, because they haven't connected. I double-check, put them in real carefully this time, making sure of each one, turn the handle again. Not a budge. I rattle the door in the hope that the lock will somehow spring loose. It doesn't bite.

'Hey! Let me have a look,' Esper says, as he pushes in beside me, suddenly getting courage from somewhere.

He checks the numbers and letters on the Visage screen and tries again.

Nothing.

'See, I told you.'

We both slip to the ground, defeated.

Then I take a deep breath. This one's not going to get the better of me. I try to figure out how my father's mind works on these things. How careful he is not to give anything away. An image of a gate flits across my brain. Of course.

'Remember the time Father had to change the code on the utility gate? Said he wasn't taking any chances. Remember what he did then?'

'Yeah!'

My hands are sweating as I punch in the numbers, this time in reverse:

ρ 6 υ 4 Θ 2 λ

I turn the handle. Please, please, please.

It gives.

CHAPTER 8

I hold my breath as the door swings open. I am in the room. The blinds are closed, so it's almost pitch dark. I can smell very clearly, though, just the faintest reminder of them, Mother especially.

'Oh,' Esper says, pushing in after me. As our eyes grow accustomed to the poor light, we can make out Seelah's favourite fluffy cat on the bivi, the one mother made from leftover fabric, her gymnastics posters on the wall, the photo of the three of us with Mother and Father when our little sister won first prize for her vaulting. They should have been destroyed. How did our parents manage to get away with that, without the Sagittars seeing them?

I pick up the cat with one eye missing. I smell it; it still has the scent of my sister. Snowy, her pretend cat, Snowy. The room, though scary quiet, makes me feel OK. We move around the walls, touching them, checking out everything. The wardrobe door opens with a creak but there's nothing there; all their clothes were burnt. The drawers are empty too, and I lie down on the bed. All I hear is my own heart going *thump, thump* in my ears. I want to cry. If Esper wasn't here I would.

'Are you crazy?' Esper shouts as I find myself pulling out the chest of drawers and lifting the bivi-base to see if I can find any trace of Mother at all. I check the top and back of the wardrobe. One long brown hair is tangled in the hinge of the wardrobe door. I curl it carefully in on itself and place it in the fold of my sock. I remember how she used to push her hair back from her eyes as she sat with us and explained how einkorn was easier to grow in the ash than wheat or why we needed to drink orgone water.

Such a jumble of memories makes me feel sick. We never spoke much about them after they were taken away because the Sagittars said it used up too many stress vitamins and we couldn't afford to lose any more.

Other than that one hair, there is absolutely no trace of her. I straighten back the bivi; close the wardrobe door so Father won't guess we've been in here. I have raised dust into the air and it makes me sneeze. As I begin to push the chest back again to its original place I see something taped to its wooden back. I pull it off. It is covered in heavy black plastic.

'Quick,' says Esper. 'I can hear the camera logging in. Leave things exactly as we found them. Out fast.'

I push the package under my jersey, grab the Visage and dash out of the room before the CWC sends the update. We try to act as calmly as possible, but I hear my heart pounding in my ears.

We sit innocently while the camera switches on and beams into the room. There stands Father in his mud-brown suit, smiling and letting us know that his Visage is not at work.

'Ta-dah! Found it.' I pull it from the side of the gel-bag.

'How on earth did it get there?'

'You must have dropped it. Anyway it doesn't matter now, we have it. And the Sagittars can get off your back.'

Esper tells him what he was doing at Academy and I tell him that Master praised me for my special assignment on the Jet Stream. He smiles at me; a real, happy smile.

'My two good boys.'

His image has barely faded when I pull the package from its hiding place.

'Let me have it!' Esper grabs it from me.

'No,' I shout at him and floor him. Father would go ballistic if he knew we were flooring, but he's not going to see us, is he? I snatch the package from Esper's hands and pull off the covering. I stare and stare at it. I cannot believe it.

It's a book.

I'm almost afraid to handle it. I've never touched one in my life. It has a dark marbled cover with the colours of green, brown and rust swirling all over it. My hand moves gently across it. It feels good.

'What?' Esper says. 'What was this doing in Seelah's room?'

'Obvious, stupid. Other than Father, no-one goes in there, no-one comes out.'

'He'll have to tell the Sagittars and where will we be then? They'll come after us.'

'Father would never put us in that danger. Fathers don't put their children in jeopardy like that.'

'If it's ever found out that he's broken the Sagittar's law on books then it's the detention unit for him, and we'll be taken in by Nanny Care.'

'That'll never happen.' I shiver at the thought.

'Put it back, put it back, please,' says Esper.

'Let me have a tiny peep and then I'll put it back.'

It's an old book, though not as old as Leonardo's one that we have just seen in Biblion. Its spine crackles with the wrinkles of time.

'Do you not want to hold it, touch it?' I ask my brother.

'No,' he says. 'You do it.'

I take the cover ever so gently in my hands and turn it. I feel the hairs tingle on my arms. Esper is at my shoulder, his breath on my neck. The pages are all discoloured. From it comes a strange smell. Page after page is full of writing.

'Yuck, it's gross,' says Esper. 'It smells like what happens when a vita-shake is left too long. Let's put it back before Father comes home and accuses us of letting off or something.'

'No, look, look at the name, will you.' We stare in astonishment.

The Book of Gold
by
Tartesah Brock

CHAPTER 9

'It's Great-aunt Tartesah's book.'

Great-aunt Tartesah was Father's grand-aunt – which makes her actually our great-grand-aunt but that's a bit of a mouthful – the aunt who gave me my nose and Esper his chin. Father did talk a little about her when Mother was alive.

Esper tries to snatch the book from me. 'It can't be. It's far too old for that.'

'Don't,' I say. 'You'll damage it. Isn't it funny that our parents never let us see this book but kept it hidden all the time? You'd think that because they loved books so much they'd have wanted to show us one that belonged to them.'

My brother goes to stand up. 'And get us all into trouble? I'm going back to my E-pistle. Something I can understand and doesn't have that awful smell.'

'You don't get it; you just don't get it, do you? It's a book, dizzard. In our house. And it belonged to one of our ancestors. Way before the Ash. That has to mean something to you. It *has* to.'

'Not if it's going it get us into trouble. And it will. I don't want anything to happen to any more of my family,' he says so quietly I can barely hear him. 'We would be better off if we had never gone into that room.'

So my brother *does* care.

'Look,' I say. 'Just a quick peek, and then I'll put it back.'

I sit on the floor and turn another page. Esper cannot bear to think he's missing out on something so he gives in, hunkers down and shuffles in close beside me. I can't believe I'm holding a book. Not behind glass, not with the Defender of the Page breathing down my neck, but in my very hands. I trace her writing down line after line. But I can't read any of it. It's illegible. I am holding the book, which is alpha, and it makes no sense at all. Letter after letter of beautiful cursive as Father would call it. But it's of no use to us. Handwriting is difficult for us to read anyway because we have never learned it. By the time we were born nothing was written any more. Mother used to get us to practise it, though, so it wouldn't die altogether. Now we just down-scroll or input onto our E-pistles and there it is on the screen. But this is a language I have never seen before. Why would Father keep something that is of no use to anyone?

I turn page after page, loving the feel of the paper in my hands as I follow each line. They are all just squidgy ink. Some of them are smudged as if the book had been left out in the rain. Others have drawings of plants and flowers. But none of the names means anything to me. I turn the final page and there's another drawing but this time it's more detailed. The light has faded in the room and I can barely see the outline.

'What could it all mean?'

'Your guess is as good as mine.'

On the next pages are a set of drawings different from the rest. Strange shapes, more writing.

'Let me see, let me see,' Esper demands. He yanks the book from me, pulls it. Half the page comes away in his hand.

'Oh, no. Look what you've done! You dizzard.'

'I'm … I'm sorry,' he says. 'I didn't mean –'

'What are we going to do now?'

'I don't know, I don't know.' He goes paler than pale. 'How will we hide this from Father? Oh no, oh no!'

'He'll guess now that we've found it.'

'Stikum tape. We'll stick it back in. He'll never know. I'll get it.' He runs back down the hall to the drawer where it's kept, in among all the other bothering bits. I hear him scrummaging through a tangle of wire and plastic and old cup handles until he unearths it. By the time he comes running back in, I've had a good chance to look at the page.

'Found it,' he says. 'Let's stick it back in.'

Instead, I put my hands on the rest of the page and yank it out.

'Oh no!' My brother puts his hands up to his face. 'You crazy or what?

'Look, there's no writing after this page, they're blank, so it mightn't be missed at all.' I'm hardly able to get the words out in the excitement. I pull away a few little jaggedy bits. 'See.' And I point to the space where the page should be. 'Unless you stretched out the binding and looked really, really carefully, like this, you wouldn't know that a page had ever been there.'

'You'd better be right. Otherwise we'll have the Sagittars, or worse, Father, to deal with. You're not getting me into trouble. It's your fault; I'll tell him you did it.'

'If I go down, you go down, so there. Let's just put the book right back where we got it and forget we ever laid eyes on it.'

With that, we wrap it up, creep back to the room and put it in its place behind the chest of drawers. No-one would ever know that it had been touched.

I take the two halves of the torn-out page and place them on the dusty floor. The ash hasn't been cleaned from here for … oh, I don't know how long. I run my hands across the two pieces, careful to iron out the jiggedy-jaggedy pieces, then match them up as best I can.

Esper holds the two pieces down while I run the stikum tape across. Dust gets stuck onto the sticky bits and the tape doesn't hold, so I have to try again. Little flags of the paper get pulled away when I do this so it's a bit of a mess. There are one or two places that have scrumpled up on me but there's nothing I can do about that.

'Do you see what it is?' My brain can hardly take it in.

'It's just a jumble of shapes.'

'No, it's not – it's a map,' I whisper, the hairs standing on the back of my neck. 'A map of Virus Islands.'

The names are written on the page in fine cursive. All five of them. I can just about read them.

'There's Galyon, the nearest. Vasuri, just beyond it. And the two further on, Mannioc and Serpens. And Colmen. Where Mother and Father came from.'

'Oh, no, we've missed Father's log-in.'

I grab the page, stuff it into my pocket and race out to the living quarters. We both just see the camera as it goes into its blue switching-off phase.

We are in HUMONGOUS TROUBLE.

CHAPTER 10

We can do nothing about it but sit on our gel-bags and start to read, waiting, the map burning a hole in my pocket. We hear Father swipe the lock on the door. He stands on the floor in front of us.

'Well?'

'It's Starn's fault,' Esper starts straight away.

I glare at him.

'We were playing with Craster and Tuan on our E-pistles and we were so caught up we –'

I hate lying to him.

'Not good enough. Just not good enough.'

'We're sorry, Father. It won't –'

'Happen again. Is that what you're going to say? How many times have I asked you? Over and over till I'm blue in the face.'

I hang my head.

'Well, since you've been so busy on your E-pistles, you'll want a little break from them for the evening, now, won't you. Come on, hand them over.'

'Ah, that's not fair. We were only –'

'You were only not obeying me, and how can we hold ourselves together if I cannot trust you?'

I don't dare look in his eyes as we hand over our E-pistles.

I remember looking out the window after Mother and Seelah's lives were taken away from us. The world was blacker than grey then. I think that was when the wobblies started in my belly. But there was something else too. It was as if lava had flowed from the volcanoes into my stomach and had hardened in its walls. Since then I have carried that rock around inside me. Sometimes it grows so big I can barely breathe and sometimes it sits in the back of my belly and I forget about it.

It's big tonight. Lying in our bivi-bags with nothing to do but stare at the walls. Without our E-pistles, we're lost. I search in my sock for the hair I found belonging to Mother, but it's gone. I've lost that too.

Father tries so hard to take over from Mother. But there were things that Mother did that he forgets to do. Tiny things. Like giving us a day off from straightening our bivi-bags on our bivis, or putting our hands in hers when they got really cold and rubbing them until we could feel the heat flowing from hers into ours. Even if we're too old for all of that now, I miss it.

Sometimes I feel really jealous of Tuan and Craster, especially when we go to visit them in their apartment and their mother is there. The room always feels warm and cosy even though they don't get any more energy coupons than we do. It's like her smile just warms up the place.

Mother's smile was the sun come out. Father tries to make the sun shine for us too, but a lot of the time, with all he has to do, its light goes out in him just before it reaches us.

I touch the map, which is still in my fist. As long as I've had memory, the Islands have been there. The Sagittars have only ever told us that they were a bad place. Now I'm not so sure. How could they be if our parents came from there? Taking the map I straighten it out as best I can and in the half-light try to make out the letters.

As I look more closely, I can see some more lines in thin black writing. This time I can read them.

'Hey, what do you think this means?'

Some of the words have been wiped out where the stikum tape scrumpled them, and letters sort of bounce around the place on me, but tracing my finger under each word I read them out as best I can.

> In the w ds are frames of gol
> A for to behold,
> If treated with the ca deserved
> Will save ou dy orld.

'That's balderdash.' Esper likes that word. He read it in a story once and now loves to use it whenever he can.

'But is it?'

'Shhh, Father will hear you,' his voice drifts off.

'Imagine if we could go to the islands.'

'You're mad; we can't do that,' Esper says. 'The zanderhags

would have you gobbled … before you … did five strokes … in the water.' He's beginning to fade.

I ignore that fear.

'Look – if we fill in the missing letters. Maybe?'

'That's just silly.'

'It's not.'

Why does my brother always have to shoot down my ideas? You'd think he was much older than me the way he goes on sometimes, not just ten minutes between us.

What if.

What if.

I look at the map again. Trace the outline of the five islands. Colmen is the third of them, bigger than the rest. Cliffs on one side, mountains on the other. I read out the broken lines by the light of the emergency lamp, trying to fill in the missing letters:

> *In the w ds are frames of gol*
> *A for to behold,*
> *If treated with the ca deserved*
> *Will save ou dy orld*

I start from the bottom as it's the easiest. Click a few letters into place: *r, ing, w* and there I have it: *Will save our dying world*. But what will save it?

I take a chance with the next line up. It could be *case* or *cape* but I'm no dizzard so I opt for *care*.

Skipping the next line, I'm drawn to the first.

Frames of gol? What's a gol? I never heard Father use the word when he talked of the island. Maybe there's a letter missing, blanked out by that smudge. Hmmm.

Then the cover of the book flashes before my eyes. *Ping. Ping.*

The Book of Gold

I jump up. Of course. Frames of *gold*. There's gold on the island. On Colmen. The arrow's pointing right at it so it must be there.

That's what she's trying to tell us. If it was any more obvious it would jump up and bite me.

Gold! Maybe not *huge* treasure, but surely enough so Father wouldn't have to worry all the time about having a job or trying to make ends meet. Ideas are swirling and swirling through my brain.

We would have enough money for food, for heat. He could spend a lot more time with us. Maybe never have to work again. Imagine how alpha that would be!

What if, what if? A plan's running around and around in my head. When we were younger and Father sent us to bivi for being bold we used to play games. Esper would turn his bivi into a rabbit's burrow or a holt, pretending his bivi-bag was a river and pillows were the piles of sticks washed up by the flood.

I turned mine into a nest. I sat there. Chirping the *svi svi* of the wren, the robin with its hundred phrases or the thrush's *trru trru trru* that sang each song twice. All their different calls. Master played them for us in Academy one day when we were studying birds. I downloaded them onto my E-pistle after that so I could learn them. Some squeaky, others beautiful, just singing to mark out their territory.

I hop out of bivi and shake my brother awake.

'Esper, Esper.'

'Whassit.'

'What if we went there?'

'Where?'

'The Islands. Found it, brought it back?'

'Found what? Brought back what? You're talking in riddles.'

'But it's the riddle I'm talking about. Listen. There's *gold* out there.'

'You can't go there. Remember the Godwins. If they couldn't do it what makes you think –?'

'If I was a bird, I could do it. So – I need to … design some kind of wings and fly there.'

He's sitting up and rubbing his eyes now.

'I suppose you're going to go out and pick up a load of feathers from the streets and use them? That's just the stupidest idea you've ever had.'

Quashed, I bundle myself into my bag and try to sleep.

In Leonardo da Vinci's notes about flying, he drew pictures of birds that depended not so much on beating their wings but waiting for the wind to carry them. They flew because of the shape of the wing, the top surface more curved than the bottom. Aerodynamics. That's what it's called. That's what made them fly. He made drawings of how they kept their balance when they were caught by air currents.

I'm shaping wings, curving a frame. Much as I don't want to admit it, Esper is right. No birds, no feathers. My mind is storming all the things I could use instead. Father's old overalls, torn bivi covers? The frame, what could I use for the frame? I'm planning, planning. If Leonardo could do it so can I.

CHAPTER 11

'Enough of the long faces,' says Father.

'We've nothing to do.'

'Oh, it's not that bad,' he says. 'Why don't we play an asking game? Throw me any question you like and I'll see if I know the answer.'

I touch the map, hidden in my pocket.

'Tell us about living on the Islands.'

'Oh,' he says. 'I didn't mean that. I meant about gravity or the Jet Stream or –'

'Please, you said anything. You always tell us not to break our word.'

Nothing for a few minutes, but then he says, 'You're right. I suppose I'll have to tell you some time.'

'What was it like?' we say together.

'Well,' he replies and I see a flicker of pain swish across his face. 'Colour. It was all colour, you have no idea when you look around at our world now. How everything then was bright, more blue sky than grey, more green trees than charred stumps, and birds, of course, in the branches, on the walls, singing their little hearts out. And everything done for the community, all people working together.'

'If it was so good, why didn't you and Mother stay there?'

'We wanted to stretch our wings to see what was beyond our island. The mainland held the promise of us both working with books. There was never a chance of that happening on Colmen. Already the storms were getting a bit worse each year. There was a lot of talk of climate change, land erosion, one or two of the cliffs had been washed into the sea the year before. The other islands, the smaller ones especially, had been evacuated by then. A lot of families were leaving. Better prospects on the mainland. Anyone who wanted to go, the smart ones, as we were called, got out. Ha! We were not so smart in the end, were we?'

'But were you not sad leaving your people behind?'

'Well, there was no-one left really; as you know your mother's parents had died when she was very young.'

She had told us about that. She was brought up by a nurse on the island who had no children herself. Sibby, I think she called her.

'There were those who were never going to leave,' Father went on. 'People whose feet were so attached to the earth there they could never move away. We stayed until my own parents, your grandparents, were dead, before we decided to make the break. Once they were gone, there was no reason to stay there. Of course it was before the Ash, so the mainland still had its beauty.

'Who was left then?'

'Friends, neighbours, some cousins who had planned to follow us, and of course –' I wait for him to say it. 'Great-aunt Tartesah.'

'The one whose nose I have.'

'And me her chin.'

He laughs. 'Yes, how can I ever forget about her when you're around?'

'Did you not mind leaving her?'

'She understood that we all had to follow our own path.'

I'm holding my breath, hoping he'll say something about the book.

'Mother said that she had a gift,' I prompt him.

'She did, all right. All the concoctions she made up, for coughs and cuts. She was the one who was called on if anyone got sick. She worked by the seasons, the way the moon waxed or waned. It was as if she could see into another world, inside people.'

He settles into the story and tells us about how she would have them all out collecting hypericum and coltsfoot and other strange-named plants that she soaked in liquids and left to draw out all the properties that were used in healing. He talks about the language they used, how they ate oats for breakfast instead of einkorn, how there were bedclothes not bivi-bags, how the vegetables were grown on the land. And there was lots of fruit.

'Those that stayed didn't want to progress. They wanted to grow crops, keep animals. Your mother and I wanted more. There were some books on Colmen but not like in the big libraries. When we left we thought we would go back some day, but you know the rest of the story.'

'Could Tartesah still be alive?'

'No, she was old even then when we left so she is well

gone by now. I remember being scared of her when I was little. But she was always kind and when we left she gave us …'

'What? What?'

'Well …' He takes a big breath. 'I was going to wait until you were older, but maybe this is the best time to show you.'

He jumps up and hurries down the hall. I look at Esper. He looks at me. Finally, he's going to show us. I strain my ears to hear him go into Seelah's room but he must be very quiet because I cannot hear that. When he comes back he's carrying a very small box. He's all smiles as he takes out the items.

No book.

'I've been waiting for the day to show you this. The Sagittars allow families to keep five items,' he says, 'and these are mine.' First he takes out a medal. 'Way before the Ash I was a four-hundred-metre winner and I still have this to prove it.' He is so proud of it. He passes it to Esper, then to me. He kept some funny bead thing; also a lead soldier that he calls General Yacobe; a picture that says 'Mud thrown is ground lost.' Whatever that means. Then he takes out a very small charm and holds it in his palm. 'Guess what this is.'

We both take it in turns to look at it. It has the head of an animal on one side and three interlocking hexagons on the back.

'Dunno.'

'This is an amulet that belonged to Great-aunt Tartesah.

See here the wolf's head. Well, that means that she had the gift with animals. She knew when they were sick or what medicine they needed. It was like she could look inside them and see what was wrong with them. Some thought she had magical powers but I think it was that she was very wise and had a sixth sense. Maybe that's where you get your interest in animals, Esper.'

Esper's face lights up with pride.

'The symbols? What do they mean?' I say, looking for him to tell me my interest in birds comes from her too. But he doesn't.

'Maybe it's time to pass it on. Maybe ... Yes, Yes. That's what I'm going to do: give you each one of my precious possessions.'

He makes us close our eyes. When we open them he has his two hands hidden behind his back.

'Pick one.'

He lets me go first. I touch his left side. He pulls back his hand. In the palm is the lead soldier. I try to hide my disappointment. Esper gets the amulet. Typical. He puts it on a string and ties it round his neck.

'It's alpha. I'm never going to take it off.'

I slip my poor prize into my pocket; try to prod Father even further for more information.

'Did she not give you anything else?'

He stares ahead as if looking out into the dark. Then he puts the other pieces back in the box, slaps his hands on his knees and stands up.

'That's the lot. Now it's time for bivi.'

CHAPTER 12

'Father, I want to train for the Kalmus Award at the end of winter.'

He is sitting with his feet in a gel bath, easing them from all the standing he does at work. I need his permission to stay late in Gymnasion.

'You!' Esper sneers. 'You, with your skinny-malink legs and scrawny arms, Coach Danarius won't even let you in the door; he'll just laugh you out of it.'

'That's enough, Esper,' Father says sternly, so I know I have his attention now. The award is for the most improved athlete in Academy and Father would love us to be more athletic. Just like he was when he won his medal. He's always wanted us to train, to win a prize like he did once. I watch his face light up at the prospect. When he gives me his blessing, my twin cannot bear to be outdone, so he says he wants to train as well. Father sends a cloud message to Coach Danarius giving his permission.

At school, we tell Tuan and Craster. They're all fired up to come with us. After final siren we go to Gymnasion, behind Academy, slip into our shorts and singlets and start. Coach Danarius is very pleased that we've all joined up.

First he gets us to stretch, to warm up our muscles. He gets us to do squats and push-ups, some more stretches. Then sit-ups, pull-ups. He has a long stick that he uses to point out the muscles that need to be worked, my trapesius, my pectoralis major and minor. 'This one,' he says, pointing to my shoulder area, my rotator cuffs. I need to be able to support my body weight. That's what my arms need to be: as strong as wings, to carry me over the water.

'You're working well. Soon those arms will take you where you want.' Does he know what he's saying? 'Keep that up and you'll get the award at the end of the year.'

I feel all grown-up inside. I never win anything, other than the gold star for my Jet Stream assignment. Esper is the one who always gets the prizes for his projects. But I know the prize I want. No good being strong if there's nowhere to use it.

Start small, Mother used to say when she would catch me daydreaming and I would tell her that when I was big I was going to be the one to get aeroplanes back in the sky. Not once did she laugh at me. No matter what I dreamed. She would stand there at the food station mixing spirulina into pea protein, advising that if I did the small things first then the big things would look after themselves.

So I do just that: start small. I can still hear her soothing voice in my head, as if she was standing beside me, while I put the finishing touches to my design. Curled up in my bivi, I wait until I can hear Esper sleep-talking to some pangolin or other and I creep out of bed. My heart is going *ting, ting* with excitement as I secretly find my way along the wall to the laundro. All our dirty linen is piled up on the floor waiting for Yellow Flag day that gives the OK for Orchard Territory to wash. Father's old white pollination suits are mixed up beside our dirty lot. I forage through them. Choose the shabbiest. Then I *snip, snip* thirty centimetres square of heavy fabric from the backside of it.

I upend the rubbish box in the corner. That's where he throws things that are too big for the bothering-bits drawer. Odd pieces of cord and bits he has collected fall onto the floor and they're just what I need. Then I crawl back to my bivi while the emergency light glows like a tiny star on the wall. Father has relented and given us back our E-pistles, so I scroll down the screen, follow the instructions and measure the cords into four equal pieces. Tie a length to each corner of the fabric, one by one, tie the cords together, then to a piece of plastic that I scrimmaged from the drawer. Finally, I tie on my prize from Father's memory box. General Yacobe. Some general from some war or other a long, long time ago. At least he is of some use now. I stand up on my bivi, take a deep breath, lift my hand as high as I can, let General Yacobe go.

He falls with a whack.

Esper jumps up. 'Whaassat, whaassat?' he slurs.

'Go back to sleep,' I whisper. 'Everything's all right.'

I slip down and pick up my parachute, check it and see the problem straight away. There isn't enough drag in the canopy. My cord is too slack so I adjust it and try again. In the emergency light I watch my little general sail down to touch the floor with a gentle *thunk*. I crawl into my bivi-bag, switch on my E-pistle and its blue glow fills the cave of my little world.

I hear you, Mother.

Yes, it's a small start.

'You look like you slept in your clothes all night, oh-son-of-mine,' Father says next morning and I nearly choke on my shake.

'He looks like that all the time,' Esper chips in. 'You just didn't notice.'

We all laugh.

'What are you pair up to?'

'Nothing.'

'You're both acting very strange lately. I just can't put my finger on it. I hope you're not both having a meltdown on me.'

'No, no,' we assure him. 'Honest.' I look at Esper. 'But we'd like to show you that we can be responsible, so from now on we'll clean our own rooms. Not have you doing it.'

'Well, this is a big day, my boys growing up.' His voice gets all croaky. 'I hope not too quickly, though. I'm not yet ready to wake up some morning and find you've flown the nest.'

I splutter into my vita-shake. Did he really say that?

Every day I'm upping and downing, stretching and rotating. Muscles expanding, contracting. My palms splayed on the floor, elbow joints doing what they are supposed to do, holding me up, my back straight as a plank, my toes holding my balance. Squats, knees groaning with the fierceness, ropes scalding my palms as I shimmy up and slide down, I leap and take hold of the bar up to my chin. Pull my body up until my head is above the bar. One, two, three, all the way until I have ten done. My arms cry out with ache as I drop to the ground, muscles burning like magma. I find the strength inside me, up and over. Run to the ropes, climb.

Then Coach takes us to the swimming pool. The water is freezing but he gets us to do lengths. Timing us as we hit one end, turn, skim through the water to the other end. He says that the swimming will ease our muscles, prevent any injury, and that the icy water will make us stronger. My skin is blue with the cold but I'm not giving up now.

So I stay awake all hours. It's easy because Father is on night shift until Interim Winds, so he comes in as we are getting up. If he saw the room now he'd have my guts for garters. Bits of fabric thrown around, circles of wire left over from the cables that are used to tie the windows down when the winds come.

Measure twice, cut once. Funny how the meaningless things your parents say suddenly come back to you and they make sense. Like right now. I can't afford to waste any material; if I cut it too short, then it's kaput. All Esper does is sneer at me.

'Dizzard! Only fit for the weirdo ward, you are.'

I'm starting on the frame, my E-pistle open at the latest design. My newest best pal Leonardo may have thought a parachute a good idea but I settle on a paraglider mechanism. I have to generate a force to overcome our weight, support us in the air. Isn't that what it's all about? That has a much better chance of carrying us. I'm saying 'us', hoping that my brother will come with me.

Omicron News is counting down the days until the Interim Winds. They come with such force that everything has to be tied down against them. Every place closes for two days, while they blow and blow and do their damage.

When they go, they leave behind the worst of winter; months and months of freezedays. I know we have to have the wind to lift us, due to the aerofoil's curved shape, so that the air passing above the wing moves faster than the air passing beneath. I'm depending on them for the lift. The lift that will take me, or us, whichever.

The first frame is a disaster, so I start again. A harness. Of course, I need one of those too. Can't do it without something to fasten me to it. There is so much to do; I'll worry about that as soon as I have this done. Curve the frame and let it lie under my bivi until I can get back to it. By the time the winds come I should be the fittest in the whole place.

Esper is struggling with the pull-ups. He wraps his fingers around the bars and tries to coax his body up with him. But nothing seems to happen. And he flops to the ground. For all his vita-shakes, he isn't half as strong as me.

'Soft worm, soft worm,' I goad him. 'If I can do it, so can you, so come on!'

He glares at me. I make a lunge for the bars, hang there for a second. He cannot bear it. His anger flares and springs right up, forces three more out of his flagging body. That's what I need to see. My brother as strong as me.

There isn't a peep out of us, our feet pedal on autopilot all the way home. Our heads dip into the pindar pie that Father has left for us. I have no memory of crawling into bivi.

Timing is everything. That's what Coach says and that's what I know. The paraglider must be finished on time. It's my only chance.

Upping, downing, every day. Stiffness slowly easing out of my joints; pain subsiding. Our pals have given up but Esper won't let it get the better of him, nor will I. The stronger I get, the clearer my mind.

My frame is coming on nicely, the canvas pulled tight across it. I start on the harness. Cut straps from the rest of the suits. By the time pollination comes around again, I'll have thought of some explanation why all Father's suits look like they've been shredded by a very angry gigantium.

CHAPTER 13

'Please, please, can we tell them, just a tiny bit, not about our plans but about our –' pleads my brother.

'Whoa! *Our* plans, that's a good one! When did they become our plans? All you've ever said was that I was only fit for the weirdo ward – and now?'

'Well …'

He doesn't know what to say for a minute. He takes a big breath, has another go, as we stand at the station hoping the pedal-pod comes soon and gets us home.

'But what about the book, maybe? Or the riddle? Tuan, Craster –they're our friends after all. We have our pact, remember, to always tell one another everything.'

While we're waiting, all the other boys from our section sweep like rain onto the platform.

'You can't,' I hiss.

'But only –'

'Don't be crazy. Have you forgotten? Their father, Mortice –'

'Their father's great fun. He's always joking and laughing.'

I suddenly feel protective towards Father. 'Well, their

father is not on his own like ours, is he? Ours doesn't have much room for fun, what with minding us and everything.'

My brother doesn't seem to see any of this.

'Well, their father is great with riddles. Maybe he'd help us with the one in the Book of Gold?'

'Have you lost your bodsticks? Think, think – where does he work?'

'Opson Stores. Checking people's food vouchers. So what's wrong with that?'

'He's just one step away from the Sagittars. What if he tells them? We might as well jump into the sea right now and let a zanderhag slip us down its gullet in one gulp.'

'But, but, they wouldn't breathe a word. I know. I trust them.'

'We can't trust anyone. Craster especially. He can't keep his mouth shut. He'd blabber it out and where would we be then? Father, think of our father. Of what they'd do to him. So, not a word.'

'Not a word about what, guys?'

A hand grips the back of my neck and I swing around. Tuan and Craster have crept up behind us.

'Oh, nothing.'

'Hey come on, guys. I heard you, my name, you mentioned my name.'

'Well, you heard wrong,' I say brazenly.

'But we're your best pals. Give us a hint, just a teeny, weeny one,' Tuan begs.

'Virus.' Esper has the word out of his mouth before I can lodge my boot on his foot.

'What about virus, Esper Brock? I suppose you –'

'Look,' I hit back. 'We were talking about something we read about the virus that killed Mother and Seelah. OK? Have a bit of savvy.'

'Sorry, guys,' Tuan rushes in, his face red.

That shuts them up.

The pod finally arrives. Tuan and I sit in the front carriage.

'Let's play mnemosyne,' he suggests.

We've just learned the game of remembering and Master has told us to practise it all the time so we can build up our memory cells.

'I'll start,' he says and rattles off: 'Run over your granny because it's violent.'

That's easy-peasy because it's all the colours that white light can be broken into when it passes through a prism. Red, orange, yellow …

But I'm distracted by Craster and my brother in the seat behind. They're whispering. I can't really hear them but as the pod slows down to let people off, Craster is promising he will show Esper how to get to the next level of Cosmology. My ears strain to find out why he would be so generous to my brother. That's the last thing he would be, because Craster always wants to be alpha. And then I pick out two words: BOOK, TARTESAH. My heart nearly stops. I swivel around in disgust. My feet come off the pedal and people start shouting at me like they always do. 'Pedal-pooper, pedal-pooper.'

But I don't care. I want to punch my twin in the jaw.

I barely wait for the carriage to pull into our station before I jump and sprint all the way home, Esper calling after me to wait, me blocking out his voice.

CHAPTER 14

Wham. With one thump I floor Esper. He doesn't see it coming.

'Ow!'

'Why ...'

THUMP

'... did you tell Craster ...'

THUMP

'... when you promised not to?'

THUMP

'Ow, ow!' he cries.

I'm strong now, strong as a gigantium. He's ready for my next attack, sees my punch coming and puts his hands up to protect his face. Balling my fist, I'm ready to have another go but, *whammy*, he gets me right on the nose. My head goes all funny. Zig-zag lines go across my forehead behind my eyes; my ears pop. I wipe my hand across my nose. Blood is pumping out of it and into my mouth.

'Now look what you've done! You know we can't afford to lose any blood, our life force.'

'Don't be such a doozy. Just do the thing with your head like we've been told to.' And he rolls out of my reach.

So I put my head back and pinch between my eyes until it's stopped.

'Serves you right. You started it. You know what Father would say to you for flooring me. About doing no harm to anyone.'

My anger is more than I can manage and I don't want to think of any of that now. My nose still stings like blue blazes as I wipe the last of the bloody blood on my sleeve. Any chance of my brother coming with me has just gone up in the clouds. So has the chance of doing a test run. My plan was to practise first on the ground, learn how to control it, practise take-offs, control the wing overhead. That's all gone now, due to his stupidity. I'll have to be ready to leave as soon as the winds start. There's no time to spare. It's Father's last night shift before Interims so there's only tonight to move the glider to a safe place until I'm ready for take-off.

Before leaving the house I go through every inch of the wing, checking out each side of the fabric to make sure there are no tears. I examine the risers, double-checking that they are well secured to the links on each side of me. Then I check the links at the end of each set. I spread all the suspension lines like a fan across the floor, check that all the loops will hold for the

upper line cascade

middle line cascade

lower line cascade

Each side is secure: Check.

Strong enough to hold firm against the strongest gales: Check.

My eyes are fighting with me to close but I force them wide open while I check the strength of the harness then try it on for size. I had made it to fit two of us, thinking my brother would come, but now it's too big so I take some stuffing from an old bivi-bag and use it to cushion any impact. I double-stitch it just in case. My fingers ache where I have to force the needle through the fabric. Just enough till I get there. I empty out my Academy stuff-sack, pack in some clothes, protein bars, einkorn and a bottle of orgone water. Ready for the morning. For the off.

I'm thinking big now, Mother.

How to take the straps into the centre. Fold the sides of the frame in on itself, first one, then the other. Scrunch it up into a roll. As soon as I've made it as small and tight as possible, I bundle it as best I can into one of Father's unused stuff-sacks.

Esper is sleeping away, mumbling as usual about crocodiles and geckos and quetzals. I sneak down to the cupboard in the laundro, pull out one of Father's old night suits, gauntlets, hood, engulf myself in them. Haul the bag onto my back. I move my hands along the wall till I get to the door, decode the lock and, in the wink of an eye, creep down the stairs. The glider weighs more than I thought, but, thanks to Coach Danarius, my back can take it.

My foot hits the street, now too dark for shadows. I pull the hood further around my face. It's cold enough tonight but nothing like it will be after Interims. I switch on the button-lux attached to the sleeve of Father's coat. Its beam is just enough to trace a line of light along the pavement so I don't trip over bits of stone that fall from the crumbling buildings that still litter the streets. Indigents sleep in alleyways, hiding from the Sagittars. If they don't die from the cold, they'll be trucked away before morning.

Only the sound of the night pod way off can be heard as I secretly make my way along the grids while workers stand shivering for their lift home from the night shift. Different departments finish at different times; people scroll in and out all through the night. My hood over my face, gloves hiding my hands, I climb in at the next stop and pedal like a man until two stops before Gymnasion. Then I jump off and walk the rest of the way.

Academy looms up from the darkness. At the metal gates there's a flicker of movement. I shrink back against the wall, flat as a pancake; switch off my button-lux. There are footsteps, a light beam spiking the dark around me. A Vigilant. Freezejam. I'd forgotten they'd been brought in by the Sagittars to patrol the perimeter. There had been a break-in during summer hiatus. One of the microscopes had been stolen and they never caught the culprit. I pick up some stones and throw them into the distance.

'Who's there?'

There's the click of his Tevlar gun.

I pick up another few stones and throw them in the opposite direction. Again a handful of pebbles that scatter in all directions. He swivels around, unsure where to attack.

I see my chance, run for it and am the other side of the gate before he can say *psittacosis*.

My aim is the back of Academy and beyond Gymnasion to the small watchtower. It was built when the ash was at its worst and the Vigilants were hired to spend days up there checking for cloud and to sound the siren to alert everyone. There's a small bunker beside it, where gazillony hubs, shin pads, helmets are kept. Academy was winner of the final game last time, so they won't be taken out again until winter is well and truly over. I sneak towards it, slip the lid off, push aside the helmets, slip the bag off my back, take out the glider and conceal it behind the shin guards. The empty bag weighs nothing now.

Here's the tricky part. Dark is all around me and I'm struggling without my little sleeve light. A stone catches my foot and it's my face to the ashy ground, knocking the breath out of me. The guard spins around, comes running, his light punching holes in the night. I'm curled, motionless, behind a bollard that divides the yard into sections, become one of them as the light beams up and down, across and over the ground. Fear is now erupting like volcanoes in my body. My heart is a set of drums in my ears and if he comes within a govey's roar of me, I'm Tevlared. I command my breath to stop, hold it all in my lungs, won't let it out, but there's a cough starting. It begins way down, I suck it back. It tries again, I swallow. *Thump, thump*, my heart beats, louder and louder in my ears. Worse than the siren, worse than volcanoes exploding, the cough bursts from me.

'Come out or I'll shoot.' The Vigilant's voice cuts through the night.

There are rules, I know. That he mustn't draw unless attacked, but we've heard otherwise. There's nothing for it but to show myself.

I step out into his beam of light. He cannot see my face. Yet.

'Turn around.'

I do as I'm told.

'So, what have we here?' he growls. 'A little man. Pretending he's a big one. The worst kind. You'll rue the day you stepped inside this gate.'

With his stun-gun in my back he takes out his messenger and calls HQ to tell them he has the culprit. I see my moment, pull myself from his grasp. He makes a grab for me, catches Father's stuff-sack on my back. Swinging my arms backwards, I slip out of it. He's left holding none of me as I run, run with my life. Take a leap for the railings as if I had Coach Danarius tapping his stick on my legs. Up and over, and land the other side, like a gymnast.

'Back here you, or I'll shoot,' he shouts.

A volley of pellets pings off the iron railings. One nips the sole of my boot as I pick myself up, spring off the ground like a runner out of his blocks.

I run

and run

and run.

The night pod shunts into the station. Sweat is running in rivulets down my back. They could siphon my heat into the grid, I'm so hot from the chase. The hood is well around my face, covers all but my eyes as I jump on. The men talk in low tones about this and that. Others close their eyes. At the next stop men are standing with their stuff-sacks waiting on the platform. Their weariness fills the night air. Two men climb on; push in opposite me to the only two seats left. They plonk their bags on their laps. I recognise that sigh.

It's Father's.

CHAPTER 15

I snap my eyes shut as Father settles into his seat, connects his boots with the pedal and joins with everyone else as feet all move in the direction of home. How did this happen? Surely his shift ends much later? That's what he's always told us – that it's dawn before he gets back.

'Well,' the man beside him is saying, 'catastrophe waiting to happen, no two ways about it.'

'Yeah,' Father replies. 'There hasn't been a foul-down in seasons. And on windmill 147! That'll scupper up the grid big time. They say a number of the men were caught in it, only just got out in time. Lucky no-one was killed, just a few broken bones.'

'If they don't get it sorted, that's layoffs for all of us. And who can afford that?'

'You're right there, Tymon,' he says to the other man. 'The Opson Stores won't exactly be all understanding and give us provisions out of the goodness of their hearts without coupons, will they?'

His friend beside him, Tymon, gets drawn in.

'I know. The last thing we need is another Black Year. And where would that leave us?

'Oh, that would be a disaster through and through,' Father says.

Tymon is nodding his head in agreement as he continues. 'No energy: no heat. No heat: no food, and if we can't eat then it's down the slippery slope. And how do we feed our children?'

'We know that scenario only too well,' Father says a little more quietly as Tymon keeps talking.

'No food and we're susceptible to all sorts. Viruses and the likes will get a hold and then where are we? But who am I telling? You know all about that, Hiram.'

Father says nothing. He knows only too well.

I keep my head down, keep pedalling so they won't draw me into their conversation. But I'm thinking. If Father's job goes then all the more reason to bring back the gold. It's one time I'm glad of the dark, only the strip lighting along the track for guidance. All I need is for him to recognise his old coat, where Mother mended the flap on the pocket, his gauntlets with the rip at the thumb, and I'm fracked. So I fold my arms across my chest, hiding the thumbs, and keep my legs moving. No-one's going to call me pedal-pooper this time.

His bag. What if there's something in the bag that identifies Father?

One stop before home, I jump off in the confusion of strangers and quickly lose myself into the shadows. Then with all the speed I can muster, I run all the way, through back grids and alleyways, to arrive at our apartment block before Father. Stairs, three at a time, I'm up and in the door while he's down on the ground, still talking to his workmate. Flinging off his coat, his gauntlets, I bundle them into the chest in the laundro, scurry into my bivi.

That's me now, an expert at pretend sleep as my ears are on high alert, waiting. There he is opening the door, plopping his bag on the floor. Then quietly he tiptoes into our room, as he does every night he returns from night shift. Tucks our bivi-bags around us. 'Good night, my two precious sons,' he says and, as silently as he came, he goes down the corridor to his own room.

Something wakes me before the alarm. I hear it. A low hum below the radar. Almost.

I hurry down to the food station. He's there, preparing our vita-shakes, getting our food ready before we head out.

'Father! Have you just come in? Are we late or you early?'

'Let me tell you about the night I had.'

Old news to me but Esper makes up for it and is all ears as Father tells us about the foul-down on mill 147.

'It's an ill wind that blows no good. It means I'll have extra time with you now, and glad of it.'

How I wish I could tell him all that I've done and what I'm planning to do. But no. He'd never let me go. That would be the end of my plans. He switches off the shake-maker and hands the shake to me.

'There was a message in my cloud-box last night from your pals' father.'

'Which pals?'

'I thought there were only two? Tuan and Craster, of course.'

I look across at Esper; he's concentrating real hard on getting the last of his shake out of the container. I hold my breath. Craster wouldn't have told his father, would he? About the book? Aunt Tartesah? The map. Oh, the map, I mustn't forget that.

'Lavvy visit,' I shout and run down the hall, pull the map out of the secret hiding place and fold it into my sock. By the time I get back, Father is telling Esper something that makes me prick up my ears.

'He wants to see me, says he has something to ask me. Funny, I haven't spoken to that man in a long time. Not since he gave me some extra dextran bars for you last visit. Maybe he has more for you. That would be nice, wouldn't it? You come home this afternoon and maybe I'll have an unexpected treat and if the winds come we can cosy up and play a game of Mancala; be all together till the winds subside. I'll drop into the Stores when you head off.' But he has that look on his face.

'You're mulling something over, Father,' I say.

'Hmm.' He strokes his chin. 'He said it was urgent, though. A few sweet bars are hardly urgent. But you know him, always joking. He'll hand them over with all this palaver and then –'

'Yeah,' we both chime in. 'A real joker.'

'Come on, now. Enough of this lollygagging. Time for off.'

I slip my packed stuff-sack on my back. Then Father walks us to the pod, telling us more about his night before and the breakdown in number 147 but that we were not to worry about him losing his job. Again.

CHAPTER 16

Tuan and I are in the laboratory with Professor Kurus. He separated Esper and me last time because we were whispering too much. My brother is now in the other lab with Craster, studying the cell walls of the inside of their cheeks. I'll floor my brother if he tells any more of our secret.

Prof is showing us the principles of condensation, how to distil dirty water. We watch it coursing through the condenser. Soon the big glass bulb of the still is bubbling away on the bench. The steam rises through the glass tube to the condenser, the vapour hitting the cold glass and reverting back to pure H_2O.

It's alpha.

Above the bubbling I hear it. Professor Kurus stares out the window and I follow his gaze to Academy's flag. Its swallow tail flutters in the first breath of wind. Its azure blue length is being picked up, it waves in the breeze and for a moment I see the star in the middle of it. Prof looks around the class to see if anyone has noticed. I turn my head immediately to my E-pistle and start drawing the round-bottomed flask of the still; record the boiling point of water. I don't let him catch my eye, but I think he knows anyway what I've seen. This is the first sign, and the time between this and the full force of the wind is maximum six hours.

A low hum is now beginning outside, as if a gigantium is searching for something. Further down the building I hear a rattle. A window not fitting tightly enough has become loosened, something slams and we all jump. The halyard of the flag outside begins to slap against its pole. Soon it feels like the walls of Academy are swaying back and forth.

The sound of the siren rips through the whole building, screeching at us, while Prof's voice is drowned out over the airwaves. He starts telling us to follow his instructions, to put our headphones away and start moving towards the door in an orderly fashion. But nobody listens. Already there is mayhem, everyone pushing and shoving and running towards the door. I see Craster in the corridor.

'Has Esper gone out already?'

'Think so,' he says. 'What's up with you guys? I asked Esper to hang on but he just bolted. Why won't you tell us what's going on?'

'Promise I'll tell you when I come back.'

'After Interims, when we're all back in Academy, you mean?'

'Course that's what I mean. What else would it be?'

A wave of bodies pushes towards the open doors. I'm being carried on the surge that is heading towards the pod depot. Last year some learners didn't get onto the pod in time and had to spend the two days alone in that part of

Gymnasion where old equipment is kept. They were in a terrible state when they were found.

Tuan and Craster are pushed on ahead of me but there's no sign of Esper anywhere. I call out his name. The wind is beginning to howl in earnest by now. Anything that is any way loose is being whisked up and blown across the tracks. Pieces of the shelter have come away and are flapping back and forth. There is the sound of the wind howling all along the track like some great beast about to devour everything in its path.

Still no sign of Esper. I call his name again but there is too much noise for me to hear anything. Someone's hood is blown off his thermo-suit and we all watch it flip and roll across the track to the other side. He puts up his hands to protect his ears. If the dust gets in they'll get infected and his hearing will be lost. Interim carries all sorts of diseases and fever. It carries the cold too and already everyone is shivering.

What I see first are the helmets, the way the spear stands up from the top, charging towards us. Sagittars. *The book.* Craster, Tuan – they told their father then. Why did I think it would be any different? They just couldn't keep it to themselves, could they? I spin around. Esper? Where is my brother? I cannot find him anywhere. All the learners are pushing towards the vehicle. The wind pushes against me with such force that for a moment I'm standing still while the others rush themselves onto the pod as they see the guards coming.

The Sagittars are shouting, 'Get back, get back. Where are the Brock boys?'

My pals are seated in the first carriage. I catch Tuan's eye. He looks frightened. Serves him right. His brother couldn't keep his mouth shut and he's landed us in this mess. But he doesn't stop at that.

'There,' Craster shouts out. 'There's one of them.'

CHAPTER 17

How could Craster do that? Betray us. He's supposed to be our pal, to mind us and save us when we're in trouble. He's a snitch. Why did I ever think he was my friend?

I don't know which way to turn. No brother, no friend. I'm colder than the wind could ever make me as I turn, scrunch down, push my way back through the boys, down on my hands and knees, crawl in and out between their legs, skulk by the wall as the wind howls and threatens everything.

'There, there,' I hear Craster shout again. Only when I look up through the forest of legs do I realise he's sending them in the opposite direction. Away from me. I breathe in. I've done him wrong. He's still a pal.

Everyone is pushing and shoving. The guards head towards the front carriage of the pod searching for us. They don't see me as I slink away, crawl along the wall, head towards the watchtower.

The wind slaps me across the face.

'Weight, drag, lift, thrust,' I growl back to it.

It just gives me another slap.

I battle it all the way to the watchtower. It's forcing me back to where I was, back in the direction of the pod, and it takes all my strength to fight it. I cling to the wall, moving alongside it, not letting it get the better of me. The sky looks like it's burning from the ash that's being whipped up. I check with my chronometer. It will be dark within an hour. When I pull open the storage box, the wind takes the lid and soon it's hurtling along the yard like a chariot. I haul out my glider, hold it tightly to me and force my way to the base room of the watchtower and creep inside.

I sit there, humming to myself not to be too frightened, the glider close beside me. Time ticking by, the wind getting stronger and I only have that short window of opportunity. They say that the zanderhags in the water are at their worst when the wind whips up like this. That it makes them angrier and hungrier than ever. If I don't make it across, then Father will have to wait nine days for my thermo-suit to eventually come to the surface. That's how he'll know. Little I can do right now; I cannot go anywhere.

The beast of a wind is getting angrier and angrier with me. I've never heard it to be so fierce. It howls around the walls and it feels like it will lift the building with me inside it. I'm stuck here for Interim time and there's nothing I can do about it. Thinking of Tuan and Craster and how they spilled our secret makes me so angry but there's nothing I can do about that either.

What would Father do if he was stuck in the same position as me? He always says that whistling a happy tune is the way he gets over being afraid. He must have had to do an awful lot of whistling when the Ash came and no-one knew if they were going to smother from it or starve. Anyway, that's no good to me because I can't even whistle. Mother used to say I'd be a great whistler because of the space between my teeth. I try to blow, to get some sound out. Nothing. Nada.

I wonder if Father's got my message yet, posted to his cloud-box, not to worry about me and that I'd be back very soon. What a great surprise it will be for him when I return with the gold! I check my chronometer by its tiny light. It's getting very close to take-off time. I search in my stuff-sack and pull out a protein bar, break a piece off and nibble slowly on it. I need to stretch my rations. They're going to have to last me way beyond the storm. I can see Esper already at home by now, telling Father my stupid plan.

I check my time piece once more: fifteen minutes left to take-off. I spit on my hands to wish myself luck. Taking out the glider, I straighten the cords so that they are not ravelled. Ah well, my brother got his chance.

It's either the lid of the store box or part of the roof that's hammering against the door, making a fierce racket. Just my luck if it's blocked my way. I grab at the door and it collapses back against me, throwing a bundle on the ground. It starts to groan.

'Starn,' the bundle says.

'Esper? What happened? I thought –'

'In, please.'

I haul him in and drag the door behind me. He lies on the floor groaning and I kneel down beside him.

'Drink.'

I open my bag and take out my water bottle. Holding his head, I make him swallow it down the little red lane. For a few seconds he just lies there. Then his eyes open and he looks around.

'Is it too late?'

'We still have a few minutes,' I reply, 'but tell me –'

'Just let me get my breath back.'

'No time for that,' I say.

He's huddled there taking big gulps of air that the wind has knocked out of him, me counting the minutes and the gusts of wind as they battle against the door. We'll lose our chance if we waste any more time.

I shake his shoulder. 'We can't stay much longer. If you're not able for it, I'll go on my own.'

That's enough to get him going, and, before I know it, he's standing up and pulling himself together. 'Not letting you go on your own. We're in this together. So what are you waiting for?'

I'm not waiting for anything; we're in this together. Grabbing the glider and the stuff-sack, I open the door again and a gust comes. It's slamming back and forth, back and forth, and then it's whipped right off its hinges. I hear it clatter against the fence and skitter along the ground. We struggle and fight our way around the back of the watchtower where there's a metal ladder that brings the men up on its roof when they need to look out. I force Esper onto the first rung, making sure he doesn't fall back on me. His feet are a bit wobbly and halfway up he stops for a minute and I think he's going to turn back.

'Keep going!' I shout.

He takes another step and I come right behind him. Another and another, until we are at the top of the ladder. It's a battle between us and the wind now and it takes all our strength not to be blown right off. We slither our way onto the roof. One after the other. The wind takes our breath away. Fighting its strength, we unfurl our glider, my belly all iqsi with excitement. There is no other way for it but the reverse launch. So I face the wing of the glider, making sure that we have it in flying position. I pull the cushion out of the harness and grab Esper. We bundle into it. It's a tight squeeze. The wind catches the wing, inflates it, all suspension lines are pulled out. I check quickly. They are all free, not one of them tangled.

WEIGHT   DRAG   LIFT   THRUST
WEIGHT DRAG LIFT THRUST
WEIGHTDRAGLIFTTHRUST

And we are away.

PART II

Islands

CHAPTER 1

'YAHOO!'

Up, up, up we go. My brother and I tucked in together, the wind whooshing under the ripstop, swelling out the cells. It whips us up just like my E-pistle said it would, the wing a glorious aerofoil curved with air above us.

'YAHOO!' we scream again into the sky. Up into the dark, the dust swirling all around. The collywobbles that were filling my stomach earlier have vanished and my heart leaps inside me like it never has before. The wind howling around us. The wing billowing, the lines taut.

Thank you, Mr Leonardo, you're alpha. YAHOO.

I look down. All the lights of my world below have been blown out by the storm but I am monarch of all I survey. I can't see where we are, only that we are flying for all we are worth. Up through the clouds of ash – we've done it. *Goodbye Orchard; goodbye Academy; Opson Stores; GOODBYE Sagittars. You didn't catch us after all.*

'See you soon, Father. We'll be back before you know it. We'll bring you back the treasure. We'll bring back all the gold when we find it and we'll be richer than kings. You'll never have to work again.'

Wind and dust and cloud drag on our lines. I pull to the left, the glider veers to the right. I pull to the right, it veers to the left. I manoeuvre the lines this way and that. We pull them together. All that training is coming into use and I'm getting the hang of it now. *Thank you, Coach Danarius.* The aerofoil plays with the wind and tells the wind what it wants to do. We are moving forward.

'Esper, we're doing it, we're on our way.'

So this is what it's like to be a bird, gliding through the sky. So easy-peasy. I relax into it, floating on a dream, one of those dreams that you don't want to wake up from. It's giga-alpha. Me with my own wings, no feathers but as good as. Now I'm flying like I always wanted to, above the Territories, this magic thing of lift and thrust, looking down on the world below, manoeuvring as if I had flight feathers, pulling forward, pulling back, veering this way and that. It's the best feeling ever.

A saucer of black covers all below. I can't see anything. The glider sails right by.

The wind blows.

We should be sailing over Gymnasion now, leaving behind Academy, then out along the tracks of the pedal-pod network until we come to the waterways. If I can keep this going and not let the wing collapse then we'll make Galyon before we can say *psittacosis*. The map has its own hiding place, safely tucked into my sock. The wind blows and blows.

But I'm controlling really well. Pull the lines as we sail along. We'll go searching straight away for the gold. Then pack it all up in the harness and be back before Father has time to get really sad. The Sagittars will be so grateful to us they won't punish us or anything because of the riches we'll bring back. We scud on and on and on. The wind blows a little stronger.

We're veering a little to the left so I pull on line five to straighten us up. Get back on course. It blows stronger again. I pull on the line. It takes a little more strength this time and the next. The wind blows and blows.

I'm getting a little iqsi now. It begins to rain, a sharp sleety rain that bites my face. Then hailstones, big wallopers of things, start to beat down on us. *Clap*, a noise like pedal-pods crashing into one another fills the air all around us.

Crash.

Clang.

Roar.

'Pull on the line!' I shout to Esper. 'Pull on the line!'

We pull. Nothing happens.

Thunder crashes, rolls each side of us, wobbles us. Then another clap and another. Flashes of light spark and fork the dark all around. Electric blue, yellow, green and red light up the sky, beautiful colours in front of and around us. Hailstones, sharp enough to skin us, slice the exposed parts of our faces. We must, we must, whatever happens, hold ourselves against the lift.

'Pull,' I shout again to my brother. 'Keep pulling.'

My breath is whipped from me by the wind roaring and spitting. It's so big, it engulfs all the space around me and makes me shiver. It's the biggest sound I've ever heard. I cannot keep it out. It has even got inside my skin and it feels like I am the wind itself, for I can feel nothing, see nothing and hear nothing but the storm. My eyes want to close but they cannot. They want to feel sleep covering me like a bivi-bag but just when I think I might doze off another huge gust whips up and I'm wide awake again. The wind is without mercy now, lashing us, skirling this way and that around us. We haven't the strength to even keep ourselves in the one place. My eyeballs are sore from the cold of the wind. We call on every muscle until our arms are nearly wrenched out of their sockets as we try to spiral against the lift. Whatever we do has no impact. Nothing. Nada. I have no control of it any longer.

'Starn, what do we do now?'

'Hold on, just hold on, we'll ride it out.' But the words are snatched from me in the whip of the wind.

It happens.

Cloud suck.

We're being sucked up into the swirl of the storm like two puppets being pulled by a giant puppet-master operating from the clouds. I am powerless as we are sucked

Up

Up

Up

No matter which of the lines I pull, it makes no difference. We are still being dragged up.

And then the cold. It hits Esper first. Ice begins to form on the shoulders of his suit.

I hear him shout something but his voice is stolen away into the vortex. I have no power against it. I breathe in, but it's as if a gigantium has sucked out all the oxygen. Esper's body begins to shake. I'm gasping for air.

'Esper, are you doing OK?'

'I, I … breathe …'

The roar of the storm guzzles my concentration into the black hole of the dark.

'Hang on, just hang on.' I reach out my hand to touch his arm and the ice has already settled on his sleeve. He has protected me from most of that until now. My body begins to shake too as we are sucked up even further. Ice is forming all over us. We are becoming ice-boys. The pain of cold hits my forehead and travels down through my body. Our limbs shake and shake as we gasp for air. We are nothing in the midst of such power. Nothing more than a grain of ash whisked up into the cloud.

So dark, so very dark.

The temperature has dropped more digits than all our fingers and toes. It's without mercy too, skinning me with its knife-sharp fingers. Shivers gallop up and down my bones. There's no way I can protect my face from the ice. I blink and realise that it has frozen my eyelashes. I close my eyes so it won't freeze my eyeballs. Sleepy, so sleepy. All I want to do is sleep as we ice over.

'Esper, stay awake! Stay awake!' I grapple with the words.

'Trying,' he says, but his voice is very weak, I can barely make out what he's saying.

'Esper.' I poke my elbow into his ribs. 'Don't let it get the better of you. Think of gold; of the treasure; think of us getting there. Don't leave me on my own.'

I get no response.

'Esper,' I shout again. But then a big thunderclap drowns my voice. It's as if it squeezes all the bones out of me and there's nothing to hold my body up. My neck curves, my arms go limp, my head is falling forward.

'Esper, Esper.' I need to keep calling him; I need to keep calling him because … because … What did I want to say? The ice cold has whipped all thoughts out of my head and I can't catch them as they fall down into the ash and the cloud. My blood has turned to ice, my brain a block of frozen flesh, as we swirl around and around, going nowhere.

'Esper.' My voice freezes before it reaches my lips and nothing comes out. The cold. Please, someone take me from this cold.

Whoosh. A sword of blue light whips by me like the Child Watch Central charging up and a screen with its eerie light is in front of my face. From somewhere back a voice calls out my name.

'Come with me, come with me,' the voice says. A girl's voice. It's stronger as it gets closer.

'Come with me, Starn.'

She knows my name. I recognise that voice. It's Seelah.

'Esper, Seelah has come for us.'

But if he says anything, I don't hear him. My sister's face is right in front of me.

Above her the stars are bright blue and red and gold. A mist swirls around her. She drifts in and out of the mist, and when it clears she's in a blue sky with her arms wide open. She's floating. Her pale white hair is like a halo around her face. I feel warmer for seeing her. In and out, up and down the dark, my little sister's voice is calling me. The cold disappears as she comes closer; her voice drinks it all away. The longing is so great, there is nothing for me to do but go with her.

'Come with me, my big brother,' she says, and holds out her hand to me.

I'm smiling.

'What about Esper?' I whisper.

'Him too,' she says.

I start moving towards her.

'STARN!' No other voice like it. It's Mother's, strong and commanding. 'Don't give up now. Remember faithfulness to getting the job done. You cannot leave your father all on his own.'

My sister's voice is calling me too. There is no ice clinging to my bones when I hear her voice.

'Pull yourself together,' Mother is saying. 'You've got to get there and back.'

'Come with me,' my sister says.

'Think of your father.'

'My brothers, come with me and we will be together.'

'Your father must not be left alone without his two precious boys.'

'My brothers should be with me.'

'Do as you're told, son. Pull on the cord. Pull on the cord.'

That's what makes me do it. When she commands like that I have no choice but to obey. My head is still too heavy to lift from my chest but it's like she's found my hand and guides it. The ice falls away from my fingers. She wraps them around the line, holds them there. I grasp on the cord, her hand is wrapped around mine as I pull again. The singing gets weaker and weaker until I can no longer hear it. Then I pull with whatever strength is in me.

We are spiralling

Down

    Down

        Down

CHAPTER 2

WHAM! SPLASH!

It's my body falling down through the hole in the sea that jounces me back to life. *OWWW.* Slivers of ice are whipped from me and splinter out in every direction as pain rattles up my body and through my head until it feels like I've split open. How can water be so hard? As I sink down through it, water bubbles out of my mouth. I try to spit it out but more just comes in and flows through my ears. I float up to the top, then down again and up. As my head breaks the surface, it hits off something solid. My harness. I must have been thrown from it when I hit the water. All around me is one big tangle of cords and ripstop, some of the lines wrapped round my neck. The tide pulls them after it and they tighten around my wind pipe, blocking it, choking me.

I grab onto the harness floating above me; it keeps me buoyed, but a blanket of fabric covers my head. It's the wing. Taking in a big breath, the fabric is sucked in with it, blocking my mouth, my nose. I cannot breathe. I'm suffocating and choking and my boots have filled up with the sea. If I don't get rid of them they'll pull me down.

I glom onto the float with one hand and with the other pull the ripstop from my mouth. Ahh! My lungs fill with air, sweet air. Then, holding tightly, I unravel the lines from around me and pull them from my neck. It's like I have been let out of a cage. I take in another gulp of air. It's a different breath as my head begins to clear. Waves gulp all around me, splashing beyond on the shore. There's a smell, too. A different smell, something I have never smelled before.

I sink again.

Next time I surface, I stretch out my hands all around me, flap the water to try and locate my brother, to grab onto him. I move this way and that but there's nothing.

'ESP–ERRR!'

Still clinging to the float, my full boots are like blocks pulling me down. I have to get rid of them. Scrambling around in the water for the strap of one of them, my good hand pulls it back and I undo it. I get the toe of the other boot behind but I have the force of the ocean fighting against me. Tired, I'm so tired, but I can't give up now and I keep pushing until I force my foot out of the final bit of boot. Without letting go of my life float I stretch down my hand and, with every part of me that I can muster, free myself of the second one.

Light is coming into the sky.

All I see is sea. Sea, sea, sea.

'ESP-ERR!'

Where did I lose him? At what point did he fall from the harness? Who took him? Did Seelah or Mother take him and not me? Why would they do that? Better that they take us both than leave me all alone. Twins are not separated. We are together, always together.

'ESP-ERR,' I call again but my voice just sails across the wide expanse of water. Blue-grey ripples all around me as light begins to trickle down. I kick my feet and stretch my hands up to float at the surface.

I look beyond to where the light is coming from. The most amazing thing is that there is clear sky, not a sign of any ash. Master was right. The prevailing winds kept it away from some places. This must be one of them. A ball of red-gold is beginning to float up beyond the distant shadows. It's beautiful. These tall shadows begin to take shape, emerge.

Trees?

Could they be trees around the first island, Galyon? Am I that close? A wave comes and topples over me and my skull gets walloped against the harness.

Lifting my head out of the water, I keep my hands, my legs moving, holding myself up just like Coach Danarius taught us. The trees! They're my target, all I have to do is get there and then I'm swishy-tailed. The thing is to propel my body towards the light. But I'm not making any headway. I'm being dragged down by my thermo-suit and my stuff-sack that's now carrying a ton of water in it. I slip my arms out of the sack and let it go, then start to unclasp my suit. All I have to do is keep going and I'll make it. A huge wave comes and pushes me forward.

Keep coming wave, keep pushing me. I have to make it. I just have to.

At first I don't know what they are, these dark blobs coming towards me. I had forgotten the warning. But then I see them, uglier and more vicious than I ever thought possible.

Closer

and

closer

they

come.

The zanderhag fish.

They're forming a circle around me. I sink below and what I see is even more terrifying. With their eyes divided in two, the top half sees above the surface and the bottom half sees below, so I cannot hide from them or from the barbs between their eyes, the toothed tongue to cut into whatever is in their path, their fins with poisonous tips moving in and out, their tails zipping through the water. I kick my legs to the surface. I cover my face because that's what they go for – the eyes. They gouge out the eyes and then they take the rest of the body bit by bit with their tongues.

They are circling, circling, circling around me.

Thrashing the water, I wallop it with my hands, open my mouth to start shouting, but the sound that comes out wouldn't frighten a dead tree let alone a coven of zanderhags. Nothing but a little piddly croak. Huge yawns of jaws snap and snap at my thermo-suit.

OWWW!

I cover my face with my hands. They start snapping at my fingers, trying to get at my eyes. But I won't let them. There they go again but my hands won't budge. Let them take my hands but not my eyes. No, not my eyes. They try to get through my thermo-suit. It's the only thing that's saving my skin now, as all these fish eyes come so close to my face, eyeballing me.

Snap.

I remember again Father saying that he would whistle when he was afraid. I couldn't do it in the watchtower but now there is nothing to lose. I lick my lips so that they're good and moist, take in a big gulp of air, curl my mouth into a circle, press my tongue against my bottom teeth and blow out through the gap. A sound comes through them like I have never made before. The finest sound ever.

Phsheeeeeeeeee phsheeeeeeee.

And again.

Pheeeeeeeeee pheeeeeeee.

I keep doing it over and over, thrashing my hands up and down in the water. My cheeks are aching, but I keep whistling across the circling fish. There isn't another bit of breath in me but I'm not giving up, not now; not after all that's happened. I fill my lungs with the breath of a gigantium and blow out one final blast. It's the one that does it.

One jaw closes.

Then another.

Slowly one fish moves away.

Followed by the next.

The next.

The coven starts swimming backwards away from me. A little bit at a time. I keep whistling:

Phsheeeeeeeee.

I don't know how long I keep doing that, but all the time the waves are pushing me forward. My feet hit something solid. I open one eye first, then the other. The zanderhags didn't get either of them. I can still see.

I'm lying there coughing and spluttering out all the water that found its way into my lungs. It streams down my nose. I turn my head and it runs out my ears too. I just lie there on the sand. My head is swarming with hailstones and lightning, with devil fish and fish eyes. Then it all goes dark.

CHAPTER 3

The first thing I notice when I wake is the quietness. There is no wind here. It's as if the light that comes slowly through the trees has gobbled it all up. Then I see red. There's blood running down my fingers. I lift them before my eyes. A huge gash runs down the back of my hand. One of the zanderhags must have got me with its toothed tongue. Only now do I feel it stinging from the salt water. My other hand is covered in gashes. Without my thermo-suit, well …

But the sand is under me. It's soft. It's safe. I run it through my fingers as I lie there and hear the sound of the waves behind me. The sun is slowly coming up in the sky and there is light all around. Soon its rays bring their warmth. Stretching out, my arms ache and I feel heat on my face. I slip off my sodden thermo-suit, then the rest of my clothes. Heat spills onto my shoulders, my arms, my belly. It's like being in a humongous energy station with all this heat coming out of it. As I lie there, the warmth courses through me, doing its magic. I check that I haven't lost any parts of me. All my fingers are there. I slip off my socks to count my toes. They're all still attached to me. And then I remember. There in the bottom of my sock is my map folded in a soggy square at the toe. I take it out very carefully. Part of me just wants to tear it up because this is what has landed me in all this trouble. But it's looking at me saying: *Open me up, open me up.* My fingers unfold it, straighten it out flat on the sand, secure each corner with some of the round stones on the beach. It's almost impossible to read. Maybe when it dries?

My socks get a good squeezing and the sea runs out of them too. Then the sun starts to do its work on them. My skin has never felt the heat like this. It's like having a cosy blanket all around my body. I walk down to the edge of the sea, a beautiful blue sea as blue as the sky. The water stings the cuts on my face and hands as I splash it all over me. Waves lap at my feet. Still there is nothing to see but sea. A few big boulders hulk out of the water. I walk along its edge, kicking the sand. Then something catches my eye. A dark bundle lying half-in, half-out of the water.

Esper.

I run.

Splashing along the edge of the water, I race to where he is. He's made it.

'Esper.'

His name rings above the waves.

'Esper.' At least he's safe. Seelah didn't take him with her. I haven't lost him. We're going to be able to explore all this together.

But it's just my boots and my stuff-sack. Further on lie the harness and the wing, as if the sea flung them after me. I slump on the ground. For one glorious moment I thought my brother was back with me, not leaving me on my own. I pick up the boots, upturn them, and the sea flows out of them. I go back to where the rest of my bundle is, turn everything towards the sun's rays and let them dry out.

A wild beast begins to growl in my stomach. Hunger starts to gnaw at me. I pull open my stuff-sack and rummage around for the rations I packed. The seawater has destroyed everything. Wrapped up in my spare winter vest is the einkorn grain. It's turned into mush at this stage but I stuff it into my mouth anyway. All I can taste is salt but it's better than nothing. I pull out the rest of the things. The protein bars are still there. The water has got into them too but my stomach doesn't care, so I tear the wrapper off one and bite into it. The stomach beast stops its growling. But there's only one other bar left and a fistful of einkorn. That won't last me any length. As soon as my clothes are dry I'll have to go foraging.

But I don't know what to do. My brother would have known. He always had the answer to everything, even if I hated him sometimes for it. Even if we fought when he called me a dizzard.

What had happened up there? Where did I go? Where did Esper go? What a dumb idea to coax him to come along. He didn't want me to go into the room in the first place. He didn't want anything to happen to me; that's what he said, but I didn't look after him. He cared and I didn't and now he's gone. Was he sucked up further into the cloud? Is he still up there? Did he fall out of the sky and I didn't notice? Was he swallowed in the big hole in the water waiting for him? Did his cold boots pull him under? Or did the zanderhags get him? Dumb idea, dumb me, thinking I could do this.

I walk along the edge of the sea again just to make sure, just to be certain that he hasn't been washed ashore. The waves lap over my feet.

CHAPTER 4

I slip on my dry clothes and, with my lungs full of sea air, I make my way towards the great barricade of green, a kind breeze ruffling the leaves. The trees are so tightly woven together, I can see no way through. It's only when I get down on my hands and knees that I can worm my way along the dark passage. Long rambling spikes with tiny daggers tangle in and out through the branches and tear at my clothes, at my hands. I have no names for them. Heritage studies never showed us these. Bet Esper would be able to tell me all about them. He knows things even Master didn't know about. These things that gash my skin and draw blood are spikers, or that's what I'll call them until I know better.

But the ground is soft underneath my knees, a cushion of green bivi-bag that covers the whole floor of the forest through the tunnel of trees. The smell that I got when I landed close to the beach is all around me now.

Green. That's what I'm smelling! I never thought that colour had a scent, but it has, and it's an alpha sort of scent, too. Gunnera never gave off a pleasant smell. It was always a putrid stink that made us cover our noses when we went past.

The trees are thick as far as I can see. My lungs fill with fresh air just looking at them. They're all so different. Not charred limbs of what once were trees. Some are beginning to have shades of yellow and gold, some even red. Taking in another big slug of air my insides grow bigger, my chest expands and there is the most glorious sound. A twittering and a chirping and a calling out: sounds that I have only heard on the Omicron that we watch at Academy.

Birds. Singing their tiny hearts out on every side. Rays of sun splay through the branches and throw their spotlight way above the canopy of branches where little slivers of light filter through.

Crawling, crawling through the undergrowth. Strong trunks give way to thinner ones. I know no names for all the leaves with different shapes. Some roundy and others long with little glossy, toothed edges. Spikers tangle themselves all around the branches. I pick a leaf and chew it. It doesn't taste anything like our vita-shake. It feels much more alive and bouncy but it's bitter, so bitter. I spit it out and wipe my mouth with the back of my hand. Green spit covers it. Father would kill me if he saw me.

The trees are folding themselves in around me. Lights flicking in and out of the wood as if some trickster is playing with lasers. Two steps are taken in the daylight, three more taken in darkness; one minute it's day, next it's night. Time is getting all tangled up on me so that I don't know if I'm coming or going. When I look back, there is nothing but a solid wall and no evidence at all of the world

I have left behind. Everything the other side of the trees is now hidden away, as if a door had closed on it.

And the sounds. They're all around me. I shut my eyes and just listen. My ears pick up all sorts of noises, unidentified animals that scurry in and out of trees. A shrill cry somewhere. The wind whispering to the leaves. I open my eyes and I see a funnel of light ahead.

Creeping towards it, inch by inch, out into a clearing, I rub all the awe out of my eyes. Esper, wherever you are, can you see this? I want to see him nodding his head. So this is what it was like, the world that Father and Mother knew. I am over-dressed, my clothes too heavy. I take my thermo-suit off and pack it into my stuff-sack. I sit down on some rocks and stare at the world of Galyon, barely able to take it all in. The colour receptors in my eyes haven't been used to this, have never had this experience, and I have to stop and rub them again. It's like a gigantium took his stylus and coloured in the grey world all around me. Tiny flowers of white and blue and red scatter through the foliage. There is the blue of the sky and the sounds of the birds. Tiny coloured flyers flutter by with their wings beating like miniature aerofoils, more beautiful than anything I have ever seen. I get up off my rock and start to follow. They fly ahead of me for a few yards, stop. Then they disappear.

Now where have they gone? I work my way down a narrow trail, flanked by spikers and stingers, pulling them aside as I try to follow the little flyers but they are gone and loads of other flyers come towards me. Then I see a familiar boot shape under the tangles. I hold my breath as I rush over. I pull at the boots but there are no feet in them. They are not even boots. Just two brown logs of wood. Esper is not there.

I take the last protein bar from my stuff-sack and take two small bites, then a final mini nibble, put the last precious piece back into my sack. My mind is not able to take in the new world, no Orchard, no steel mill, no granary. No grids of streets, no pedal-pods, just green and growth and spikers and flyers.

'Espeeer, Espeeer.'

But not a sound. Not a squeak, just the rustle of leaves around me, the birds. With all that noise they are making, would he hear me or I him? The path forward seems to snake endlessly into the wood. Trees flank each side like the burlies in the Sagittars. The ground underfoot is soft and yielding, except in places where tree roots surface and criss-cross like pedal-pod tracks. Easy to trip on them. I watch carefully where I step but before my foot hits the ground, I've been flipped upside down.

I'm dangling from my left ankle. Blood hurtles into my brain. Everything is swirling round and round. My stuff-sack slips from my shoulders, and it thuds to the ground. Then I hear the stomach-curdling growl.

Open one eye, then the other.

I'm looking down the throat of something fierce. If this is the little red lane that Father used to try and encourage me with, well he'll never use that phrase with me again. Open jaws. A flaming cavern flanked on each side with bloody incisors that would easily take my head off in a single bite.

Eyes blaze above a black snout. Swinging round and round, I return to the spot where the teeth are still there, long as daggers. Sick is churning in my mouth waiting to puke out. All the teeth have to do is close on my head and I'm a goner. I squeeze my eyes shut. A trap and I'm the dizzard that stepped into it. Maybe that's what happened to my twin. Stupid me, thinking that I could follow Tartesah's map and find the gold. 'Esper!' I try to scream but no sound comes. The animal lifts its head up and howls.

'Enough, Veltor, enough.' A voice gravels from behind me. The animal stops growling.

'What have we here?'

I open my eyes to see a man that looks like a walking tree trunk with clothes the colour of bark. There are the two light spots that must be eyes and a slit for a mouth. He's saying something again to the animal. And it hunkers down beside him.

HE-LP, I shout inside me but the cry falls out of my mouth onto the ground. I continue to swing back and forth, while my head's about to explode any minute. Bright colours flash through my mind and little pings of light burst upon my brain. My heart is upside down and it's like the blood is going in all the wrong directions.

'Who're you?' the man asks.

He touches the rope and I swing around again. Then he reaches across, grabs my feet and steadies the rope. He lifts me up, scrunches me under his arm, unties the rope from the branch and plonks me straight on the ground. Fluid sloshes around in the canals of my ears. Slowly they begin to balance out, and only when the ringing stops do I open my eyes.

'Name?' he bellows at me.

The animal by his side sticks close to him, its teeth still bared.

'Starn,' I whisper.

'Speak up,' he roars, and I'd swear the ground rumbles beneath his feet.

'Starn,' I say again, more loudly this time. I see his lips move behind the hair as he sucks in strands of it.

'What territory?'

'Orchard.'

'Hah, pollinators. What you think, Veltor? Will you eat him or will I?'

The fierce animal looks up at him and snarls.

The man laughs. 'Veltor says he won't eat you. You're not tasty enough, you're only sap, meat-sap, not tasty.'

He walks around me, mumbling to himself; the animal follows him, sniffing at my ankles, and I'm shaking now, shaking all over. I look up at his hairy face and his teeth are just stumps worn into the gums, surrounded by grey beard and hair on his cheeks. He has a dirty animal skin over his shoulders and a skirt of something similar. His feet are wrapped in the same sort of hide. Malfas. That's what he says his name is. He smells.

I want to ask him if he's seen my brother, but I'm afraid. I could already be looking at him inside the animal's belly.

CHAPTER 5

Huge walls of stone that millions of years ago had been spewed up by a giant from under the sea pile up on each other all around me as Malfas pulls me after him, the rope digging into my neck. I don't know how long we've been walking. I'm not sure what I am more afraid of, the rope chafing my skin or the heat of the animal's breath, scary hot on my heels. Malfas slouches and grunt-mumbles like an animal too, his breath laboured, taking no notice of the skittering movement in the undergrowth.

Roots of trees bulge out of the ground. I trip-trup on them and Malfas growls at me as he waits for me to pick myself up. He continues to pull me towards an incline.

Up and down, up and down, over rocks, we move into the darkness, the animal's breath burning my ankles. Malfas pulls me through a narrow pass with rocks covered in moss, water dripping down through them. Out of every little crevice there are all sorts of plants growing, I can barely take them in.

Some places are covered in the softest green, others are just grey stone. No way can I slow down because if I do he yanks the rope and the life is choked out of me. Veltor now takes the lead and looks back every so often to see if Malfas is following. Some of the path has been washed away by rain, and we have to walk very carefully; some of it has dried up where the sun hits it and little flowers with shining faces look up at me, so bright they almost hurt my eyes.

We trudge through more narrow gaps of stone. Veltor comes to a stop at a hole in the rock. He dips his tongue into it and I hear him *slurp, slurp*. Malfas follows, cups his hands in, draws them to his mouth. Then he lets me lie on the edge. I make a bowl of my hands and take a big slug of it. It tastes better than all the orgone water I have ever tasted.

I drink and drink and drink.

Shadows play games with the land all around. We start walking again. I don't know whether I'm dreaming or not, but little by little, the trees seem to be getting taller and taller all the time, until now they are hitting off the roof of the sky, leaving us as nothing more than specks on the ferny floor.

When we come out into a clearing Veltor stops and looks up to the top of the rocks. Something moves.

'What is it?'

'Horned animal,' Malfas says. 'Veltor likes them. Keep him fed.' The horned animals look down from the tower of stone, as if teasing us, then scamper away. Veltor doesn't show any interest. His belly must still be full. Good news for me.

We file through another endless narrow pass of stone. Trees shadow each side. Only wide enough for a body or a horned animal. There is a different smell now, a funny smell that I don't recognise either. Veltor sniffs all around. Malfas sniffs.

'Animals here,' he says, then points to the little circles of droppings on the ground.

Every now and then we have to stop for Malfas to check on traps he has set in the undergrowth. He puts the rope in Veltor's mouth while he lifts up the trap made of twigs. No chance I'm going to run from them, the hairy man in front of me, a snarling animal behind, in a space so narrow you couldn't swing a govey.

Two of the traps have small brown creatures in them; he pulls them out. I see them quivering in his big hand as he turns the neck in each of them; a small crack and the eyes go dead. He ties them to the waistband of his skirt.

We move on again, climb up some rocks to a hole in the incline, the rope still in Veltor's mouth. Little scramblings in the greenery. Birds overhead distract him but he doesn't let go. He just holds tight. My legs are ready to fall off but we keep walking until a gaping hole appears between two huge boulders. Malfas pulls back a curtain of hanging ivy.

'In there!' he says in a voice that is closer to the growl of an animal than anything else and pushes me into the dark. It's as black inside as it is light outside. I can't see much, my eyes adjusting again to a totally different world. Malfas takes the rope from my neck and ties it around my ankle, then wraps it around a spiky boulder by the door. Veltor flops beside it. I am surrounded. The ground is littered with shells; not goober shells from the peas we ate at home.

'Sit.'

I sit.

Malfas drops the snare creatures on the dusty ground beside a circle of stones with a snake of smoke coming from them. He shakes out the coals; there is a spark of red still in them. He throws a bundle of small sticks onto the flames. They smoke for a little while and it blows in on top of me, making my eyes water. But then there is a flame and another. Soon they catch fire and are let burn away until they are glowing embers. He takes the animals and slits their bodies with a stone sharp as a dagger. He cleans them out and throws the innards to Veltor, pulls out a stick and spears the skinned bodies on it, then hangs them across the fire. He sits there turning the stick.

I crouch by the light of the fire, waiting. He turns the stick again. My mouth waters, the smell is like nothing I have every smelled. *Rumble, rumble* goes my belly.

Malfas turns the stick one more time, pulls a bit of meat off with his big hairy hands and sinks his teeth into it. Pulls another bit apart and feeds it to Veltor. Then he breaks off a bone and passes a piece to me.

'Eat.'

This is what Mother and Father used to talk about all the time. Meat. I cannot wait, my stomach crying in anticipation, just like the big animal in front of me, drooling. Nothing that I have eaten in my whole short life has tasted like this, though Father tried to explain it to us.

Not like the goober steaks or einkorn burgers or anything else. I chew and chew on it until, slurp and slip, it gizzles down.

Then he passes me a wooden cup. I drink.

'How did you get here?' he growls.

'We made a glider.'

'Glider?' He starts to laugh, and bits of cooked meat sputter all over Veltor, who licks them away in an instant. 'You say "we"?'

'Yes, me and my twin. He was with me.'

More bits of food are stuck into his beard too and he sucks hair and all into his mouth.

'Two of you,' he says, 'and where is the other?'

'There was a storm. We were dragged up into it.'

'Ah, cloud suck. Not good.'

'We fell into the sea and my brother, well …'

'Hmm, one survives. The other – not much hope with zanderhags; not even this much,' he says, and takes the sucked bones out of his mouth and throws them to the animal.

Gulp.

Gone.

'Is he a dog?'

'Wolf.'

Esper should be here for this too.

'Found him when he was a cub. His mother was killed.'

Suddenly I feel a little ache for the fierce animal.

'Needs lots of meat. Fed him from my hand since he was

a baby, so he likes me now. But he's still a wolf. Always a wolf. Don't forget that.'

As if I would!

'A glider,' he says again, stroking his long beard. 'You make me laugh. Two little boys getting the better of the Sagittars. Do you hear that, Veltor? Funniest thing ever.' He slaps his knee and the wolf gives a little howl.

They're laughing at me.

'And why did you want to come here?'

'Just to see.'

'No-one comes just to see. Out of bounds, you know that. All in Orchard know. Don't they, Veltor? Come on, out with it, or this wolf here might decide he would like a bigger meal.'

I look at the animal. His smell is as vicious as the big teeth. His black snout quivers, his amber eyes glow but most of all his sabre teeth are ready and waiting. I rub my neck where the rope has been.

'We're searching for something.'

'What might that something be?'

I think of the map hiding itself in the glider. The wolf is too close.

'Treasure,' I whisper.

'Speak up.'

'Treasure.'

'What kind of treasure?' he says, holding Veltor by the neck.

CHAPTER 6

'Gold,' I say.
     'Louder!'
     'GOLD.'

'Ah. I see.' He rubs his hand through his long beard again. 'How do you know about the gold?'

The amber eyes of Veltor are staring at me, the black circles around them scarier than anything I have ever seen before, especially now in the evening light. There is nothing for it but to talk.

'A book. We found a book.'

'Don't lie to me,' he roars. 'How could you find a book? They're only in Biblion or the ones the Sagittars have.'

'But we did. We found it.'

'Where?'

'In a room in our apartment where no-one ever goes.'

'And what did the book say?'

'That there was gold on Colmen.'

'Not Galyon?'

'No, not Galyon.'

'You sure, not Galyon?'

'I'm sure.'

'How do you know that?'

'I saw it on the map.'

'What else did you learn?'

'I don't know, really.'

'How's that?'

'Most of it made no sense.'

'What you mean?'

'I couldn't read it because it was all gobbledegook. The riddle was the only thing we could read but it made no sense.'

'A riddle?'

'Yeah, and the map.'

'Where's the map now?'

'My brother has it,' I lie.

'And the book?'

'The Sagittars have probably taken it by now; they were coming to capture us when we took off.'

'And the riddle, what did that say?'

'We didn't really understand it at all. Esper memorised that too. It was his job to memorise it and now he's gone.'

I hope the wolf can't smell lies.

'You're more savvy than all the Sagittars put together. I've been here two years, only goats, ibex, wild cats, weasels. No sign of gold. The only one I speak to is Veltor. I'll make some light. Then you can tell me the whole story.'

He takes what look like hollow stones filled with fat and lights the little wick in the middle of them. Now I can see where I am. A high vaulted ceiling with all sorts of shapes around me. Long swords of stone hang down from the top and spear up through the ground. I see piles of bones and bits of broken pottery thrown around that must go back a long, long way. Back to the ancients. Up in the nooks of the ceiling there is a flapping of wings.

'What's that?' I shiver.

'Bats.'

I watch them in the half-light as they all fly out through the entrance of the cavern.

'Night creatures, heading off to feed, they'll be back at dawn time.'

The cave is huge. There's no telling how old it is with its drawings of red and black scrawled on the stones. The head of a horse; the horned animal like I saw on the top of the ravine; a flying creature.

He holds the lighting cup in his hand and moves it around.

'See,' he says. 'Listen.'

He pounds the ground with his foot. A rumble like an earthquake fills the whole chamber and I think the underworld of stone is going to tumble down on top of me. He waits until it settles, like a huge beast stopped growling.

'Hollow underneath. Just beyond this is a hole, a cave-lake. So now you know, no funny tricks or you'll end up there.'

He brings me back to the fire. It glows and radiates heat all over the cave. He takes the outer skins off his shoulders. And then I see it. The earth-suit that Mr and Mrs Godwin designed.

My voice can barely let out the words.

'Where did you get the earth-suit?'

'Veltor brought it back. Other things too he brings but they're no good. This is the only one not chewed by zanderhags.'

CHAPTER 7

'Wake up! Wake up!' Esper shouts. Light pours in through the mouth of the cave. My brother is looking down at me, shaking me awake. 'Come on,' he says. 'Let me show you.'

He moves away, beckoning me. Jumping out of my spot, where Malfas told me to bivi down, I stir myself and follow him to the mouth of the cave until I am yanked back by the rope. Dragging myself as far as I can, I watch as he walks over the stones, dissolves into the morning cloud that hangs over the mountains. He's gone. I look around the cave but there's no-one there.

The smell of animal is overpowering, my stomach is sick and heavy as a rock from trying to digest the rich flesh of last night's meat. Dust, wolf hairs tickle my nose, the mound in the corner still sleeping on, undisturbed.

A whizz above my head and little dark things dart past me into the cave. The bats are coming back after their night out. The sun comes up beyond the rocks, its brightness almost blinding as I try to take it all in. Such colours, like the rainbow that Master taught us. Reds and yellows and greens, most of all. There couldn't be enough names for all the shades. Birds flit from tree to tree, calling to one another, singing more beautiful things. The sun is burning the mist off the mountains. Spectacular flowers have their faces turned towards the light. There are branches with red spheres of fruit hanging from them. So red and juicy looking. Soooo tempting. My hand stretches and picks the bright things.

'STOP!'

It's Malfas.

'Poison.'

I drop it like a hot Sagittar.

'Did you eat any?'

'No.'

If you had, they would kill you quicker than a zanderhag, and more horribly.'

'Thought I saw my brother, but he's gone again.'

'Dreaming, you're just dreaming after snare-meat feast.'

I look around but there's no sign of his pet.

'Hunting. He goes for the day, comes back when his belly is full.'

He puts his hand into the pouch at his waist and pours something onto the ground.

'Stonefruit. Eat.' He takes a piece of flint and cracks the shell, scoops out the inside with his long dirty nail. 'Here.'

He throws the stone across to me. The sound of flint on shell rings out around the valley and echoes back to us. I follow his example, crack shell after shell, scoop out the fruit and pop it into my mouth. My mouth takes a little time to settle into the taste. They are much crunchier than pindars. Then he passes me some black balls of bumpy fruit – blackfruit he calls them. I don't know if I like the taste at first. Vita-shakes, proteins are what my mouth is used to. Little by little I let them settle on my tongue and swallow down the juicy sweetness. Why did the Sagittars want to keep all this from us? Why would they do that, when there's enough food here to feed our whole territory and maybe even others, food that's a lot easier to grow than we're getting now? How could they be that cruel!

'I won't run, I promise, if you just take the rope from my leg.' I rub the skin where it is chafed.

'When Veltor gets back,' he says. 'His jaws are better than any rope.'

He lets me outside the cave and ties the rope to a tree within his view, orders me to pick sticks that have fallen to the ground. With the leeway he has given me, I do as I'm told, gather them into little mounds, then pile them into my arms and bring them back to the fire. He collects bigger ones further off, drops them at my feet. I keep at it as the sun moves around the sky, breaking them into smaller pieces and piling them up near the fire pit.

My brother is right before me, in my mind's eye. I imagine his dark hair and his big grin and more than anything I want for him to come back.

When the evening brings the chill with it, Malfas starts the fire. He rubs a bow with a cord against a stick, the friction creating enough heat to make the twist of dry grass beneath the sticks begin to smoke. He blows on it and a tiny flame erupts. It gets bigger and bigger. A crackle of flame catches the sticks and we have a fire. He takes an old piece of charcoal and goes to the wall with all the markings on it. Draws a new line beside the others.

|||||||||||||||||||||||||||||||||||||||||

'Have you only been here this length?'

'Huh, look here.'

He brings me to the other side of a wall of rock, shines his lighting taper up and down. Lines and lines of the same length cover it, so there's no more room. That's an awful long time to be in one place.

'Two years I've been looking for the gold. Saw the files on the Sagittars' Lexicon system, when I was trying to fix a breakdown, saying there was treasure on the Islands. They were lying to everyone about the viruses when all they wanted was the gold for themselves.

'Which island did it say?'

'System crashed before I could get to see any map. So just guessed it was Galyon. Maybe there was more information that was hidden from me.'

I'm not going to start a day-log. I don't plan to be hidden away in this cave any longer than it takes to find Esper. And I will find him.

'The gold is not here. It's on Colmen. If my brother was here he'd show you the map, prove what I'm saying.

We have to start moving on straight away.' Though I am thinking, *How can we move on with Esper still missing?*

'Hmm,' he says, as if he's hatching a plan. Or just playing games with me.

No sleep will come.

Veltor is sleeping, Malfas snoring. He talks out in his sleep but it's hard to make out what he's saying. I listen carefully, trying to decipher the words. Again and again he says it. It sounds like 'Koben'.

CHAPTER 8

'Can we look for my brother tomorrow?' I ask the following evening.

'No good – he's well gone now. If he's in the sea, then there's no hope.' He spits into the fire.

But there's part of me that doesn't believe him. Mother said that twins are connected in a way that no other people are. We know what the other twin is feeling. Sometimes when I would have collywobbles in my stomach he would say he had them too. And often we would have the same dreams in the night. When we'd wake up, he'd tell me he dreamt he was in the tepidarium full of brightly coloured fish, and I'd be able to describe exactly the same ones, their colour or size. I won't believe he's gone until he's gone.

'So, how did you make your glider?' Malfas asks, and I tell him the story bit by bit, about the code to Seelah's room, finding the book, following Leonardo's plans.

'What's it like back there now? Sagittars still making a mess of things?' he asks. 'Still thinking they can get us out of this muddle with their stupid rules and their silly ways and not knowing what they are doing?'

'Father says that about them too.'

'He'll be in detention unit by now. They'll have sent

their burlies to pull your place apart and found the book. Then they'll be sure about the gold. It's only a matter of time before they finish their sky machine. It's surprising they haven't got here by now. If you can do it, then they can – but then again, why should they? As I said, being in power doesn't mean they're smart. Indigents could do a better job.'

I try to block out all the stories I've heard. No-one comes out of detention unit. Maybe Father'll be able to tell them where the gold is because he lived on Colmen and they won't be too hard on him.

'Did you get here in a glider too?' I ask him.

'No, a raft.'

'If you got here by raft, why didn't the Sagittars try that? Instead of making their sky machine.'

'They did, in the early days, three rafts one after the other, capsized, zanderhags had a feast. So they decided sky was safer. I was lucky, just very lucky they didn't get me. I knew from files that the islands themselves weren't dangerous. So sailed this way. Raft washed up onto this one. Am two years searching now and no gold, so you must be telling the truth. It's time to move on to the next one. Since you're such a smarty pants, you can help.'

'If anyone can find the gold, it's Esper,' I say.

He rubs his fingers through his grubby beard. 'We'll see what the morning brings.'

We sit there, watching the flame, throwing more sticks on it when the others turn to ash. Soon there is a steady glow and he prepares the bird he caught in one of his snares. He plucks all the feathers off it. Slits its belly and throws the innards aside. How many times have I dreamt of seeing a real bird, never thinking that this could happen to them? But I am hungry again so I try to block out that thought.

'When will Veltor be back?'

'When he smells the bird.'

I sit out the closing day. Malfas is right, for before the sun hides itself, the wolf comes loping towards us. His jaws are full. Whatever poor animal got in his way is no more. He comes right up close to me. Blood drips from his mouth as he drops his prize at my feet. It's a boot. My heart stops. It's Esper's. I go to reach for it but Veltor growls, snatches it back and goes to the other side of the fire, his paws securing it for himself.

'Can you take it from him? Please.'

'Finders keepers.'

'Where would he have got this? Does he go as far as the beach?'

'No, not there. He don't go beyond the pass of stones without me.'

'How would he get it, then? Unless my brother got this far? He could still be alive. We've got to go search for him. We have to!'

'You see this place: it's a maze, no path, no place to look for him at all.'

My brother's boot is in the wolf's lap. Crawling to the back of the cave, I curl up on the bivi-skins. Blood on the wolf's mouth fills the space when I close my eyes. My brother's blood. Night dreams are full of him, his head bleeding, his leg broken, caught between two stone clefts. The film plays over and over again in my head, so clear there's no way it isn't real.

CHAPTER 9

I wake, and the nightmare hangs around my neck like the old rope around my feet. I try to shake free of it but it's no good. I can still see Esper caught between the rocks.

I explain my dream to Malfas. 'We have to get moving before the Sagittars come. You said it yourself, they'll have taken to the air by now. We need Esper. Please let us look for him.'

He cracks a few more stonefruit and pops the kernels into his mouth, stares at me under his bushy eyebrows. Then he turns to the wolf. The animal still has Esper's boot clasped between his claws.

'No creature goes outside the trees, so it can't be the beach, it must be inside the rocks.'

I inch forward but pull back as Veltor snarls his scary teeth at me.

'Can we please have one look?'

Then Malfas picks up the boot, sticks it under the wolf's nose. 'Come on, show us.'

The animal lifts his body, stretches out his front paws and leads us out of the cave.

'Can you take the rope off me, please? You can put it on again when we get back.'

Malfas loosens the cord from my ankle. He then picks up a stick. I do the same. We follow, back through the pass of boulders, using the sticks to search the undergrowth for a clue, any clue.

'Esper, Esper,' I whisper over and over again, sending him the signals to keep him alive, 'we're on our way.'

My dream is still a living picture before my eyes. What if another animal has already come and torn him apart? What then? My nightmare comes right into the day, the scenario more and more frightening as we trudge along, the birds flitting across our path, squawking and chirping. Malfas mumbles all the way as if he is talking to someone, stops every now and then to pick blackfruit off the spikers. This morning I've no appetite for them.

Veltor is a few strides ahead of us, in and out of the rocks, squeezing through crevices. There is something familiar about the place as he manoeuvres his frame through two narrow boulders. We follow, searching on every side, using our sticks to check under spikers or the large patches of stingers that are all around.

It happens so quickly I nearly trip over him: my brother lying face down on the morning grass.

'Esper, Esper!'

'Don't touch him.'

'But …'

Malfas goes over and leans down beside him. He puts his fingers to Esper's neck.

'Still breath in him, that's good.'

He's alive. Alive! My brother is alive. My heart does somersaults, and some part of it that was broken away comes back to fit into its proper place again.

Malfas lifts Esper up and slings him over his shoulder. His dark head hangs down the big man's back like a sack of sticks. Malfas strides away with him, Veltor at his heels, licking the fingers of Esper's hand, which falls limply against Malfas's back. I have to run to keep up with them. They don't waste time but keep walking up over the stones, down the valley, through the overgrowth, around the undergrowth, up the incline, before we eventually arrive at the entrance. The big man takes my brother from his shoulders and places him carefully on the pile of skins at the back of the cave.

There's a gash on the side of his head. Blood encrusted on it. One boot still on; the one that Veltor brought to us now thrown on the ground beside him. Is that why the animal brought it? To let us know?

'Help me get his clothes off,' Malfas orders, and lifts him up, while I pull his arms from the sleeves, as gently as my clumsy hands can manage, then take off his trousers and top. His chest is all gashed and torn. Did he have the zanderhags attack him too? He starts to shiver and shiver and Malfas rushes to the corner and grabs more goatskins to wrap him in. The amulet is still around his neck. Malfas sees it.

'What's this?'

'It belonged to Father. Please don't take it.'

He starts to go through the discarded clothes, item by item, empties out Esper's pockets. All he finds are a soggy protein bar, a piece of wire, a token from a day out at Biblion.

'Map, where's the map?'

'It must be in there somewhere.' Jumping up, I pull the pockets apart. 'Must've been washed out by the force of the sea or when he was attacked.'

He mumbles to himself as he throws Esper's clothes in the corner. I don't let him see my eyes.

All night I sit on the ground beside my injured brother, watching him, not able to hear his breath it's so faint, trying to block out the other sounds. Malfas snoring, still making the sound 'Koben, Koben,' the breathing of the animal, my own chest going up and down, the outside sounds that I don't recognise, a *hoo, hoo, hoo* somewhere in the trees. But not a whisper from Esper. No talking in his sleep. No thrashing the hands that I have known all my life. Nothing. Nada. I check him again. With my ear to his chest, ever so faintly, I feel its rise and fall.

Only then does sleep come and by the time dawn breaks through the entrance, Malfas is raking the coals, roasting some meat for breakfast.

'He's still alive,' Malfas says. 'That's something.'

CHAPTER 10

'No going anywhere, now,' Malfas repeats with a laugh as he goes off for the day with Veltor. Even if I could untie the knot he knows I'm more tied to my brother than I ever was to this block of stone. They head off down the slope and I curl up on the ground beside Esper. Only for the slight rise and fall of his chest, he's not there at all.

'You'll never guess where we are,' I whisper in his ear. 'On Galyon.'

No reaction.

'The first one on the map.'

Still no reaction.

'There are all sorts of wonderful things here. Things you only dreamed of. You've got to see the animal skin you're lying under. Better than any earth-suit. Can you imagine that? There are lots of other animals here too. We need you to wake up to tell us the real names, but the best of all is … Come on, guess.'

His silence bounces off the walls of the cavern.

'A wolf. Honest. Cross my heart and hope to die in a cellar full of ash. Called Veltor, with a black snout and golden eyes. Like on your amulet. We eat birds and he eats horned animals. Malfas calls them ibex but he could be making it up. Come on, this is your big chance to shine, you can't miss out.'

I'm wasting my breath on the empty air.

The wolf returns from hunting before Malfas. He comes straight to my brother, nudges me out of the way with his snout and lies down beside Esper. Nothing for me but to shift to the front of the cave to look out at the world that has now become my prison home. What can I do? Where can I go?

When I head back in to sit by my brother's side, Veltor is licking his hand, his big raspy tongue slopping over Esper's fingers. Then he licks his face and he keeps doing it until the most marvellous thing happens. Slowly my brother's eyes open.

'You're back, Esper. It's me, Starn.'

'Who?'

'Starn, your brother.'

'I don't have a brother. Where am I?'

'On Galyon Island; the map, remember.'

He says nothing.

'Stop messing, you know who I am.'

But he just blinks at me. 'What happened?'

'You fell out of the glider.'

'What's a glider?'

'You know very well it's …' But the most awful feeling invades my stomach. He's not fooling. He really doesn't recognise me.

He puts his hand down and rubs Veltor's head. The animal licks his fingers again.

'This is Veltor. He's a wolf, imagine!'

'I know,' he says. 'Veltor's my friend.'

'How do you know?'

'Everyone knows.'

What does he mean by that? He must have got a terrible blow to his head to be thinking that way. He puts his arm around the animal and Veltor continues to lick his hand. In a little while Esper sits up and the two of them move to the entrance.

While we wait for Malfas to come back, we sit by the door of the cave, me on one side, Esper on the other, the animal resting beside him, my brother rubbing the animal's ears. I watch the birds fly from tree to tree, wings outstretched. Magic. The blood has dried on the side of his face but he still looks like he has been attacked by zanderhags.

'Do you really and truly not know who I am?'

'Will you stop asking me that? It hurts my head, smelly.'

He's right. I sniff the skin on my arms. I haven't washed since my bath in the sea. Mud on my hands and feet, sleeping on the animal skins, grease from the fatty meat, all have left me as dirty as an indigent on the grids of Orchard.

CHAPTER 11

One day passes like the other, waiting for Esper's wounds to heal. He wakes each morning looking stronger and stronger but still he has no memory of Orchard. The gash on his head is healing well, his chest has a few scabs that he picks at but they're getting better. I make some marks on the ground, drawing the layout for gazillony, the hubcaps, scoop out a hole for the scoring chamber in the dirt.

'This is what we played, remember, before the worst of winter.' But there's no light of recognition at all in his eyes.

'Sure,' he says, and kicks the dirt back into the hole.

'Hey, why did you do that?'

'Just because.'

There seems to be no way of getting through to him. He's so not like my brother any more.

'Do you remember nothing about us?'

'About what?'

'About before, about us together, Father, Mother, Seelah.'

'Who's Seelah?'

'Our sister.'

He makes no comment, so I bring him to the back of the

cave, pull out my stuff-sack, show him the glider, with its harness and all its lines. But he shows no interest. He turns and rolls over to play with Veltor. They are inseparable, more like brothers than we ever were.

'Esper is very good with the animal,' Malfas says.

'But he only ever saw them on Omicron, or read about them on his E-pistle.'

'He has special powers with him. Veltor, come.'

The wolf doesn't seem to hear Malfas but continues to follow Esper, who wanders in and out through the mouth of the cave.

Malfas stretches out to grab him; the animal turns and snaps at him.

'You see how they can turn,' he says to me. 'You can never trust them.'

'I know. Once a wolf, always a wolf.'

CHAPTER 12

Malfas bends down to tighten the rope around my ankle. He's smelly. Mother would have thrown him in the public baths if he came within a govey's roar of her. I wait until my brother has headed down the hill with the wolf.

'Who's Koben?' I ask.

He jumps back from me as if I'd struck him. 'Where did you hear that name?'

'I … I …'

'Do I have to say it again, do I? Who told you about Koben?'

'I hear you call it out … in your sleep.'

He sucks his beard into his mouth. 'What?'

'Yeah, at night when you're sleeping.'

'Every night?'

'Don't know, but any time I've been awake.'

He slumps down on the ground beside me, all the energy squeezed out of him.

'Oh,' is all he says for a few minutes.

Then he leans over and tightens the rope around my ankle even more, turns and tramps out of the cave. Why did I open my big mouth and make him angry? What do I even care who Koben is?

The day stretches out lonely before me. For something to do I drag myself and my rope to the back of the cave, pull out my stuff-sack from behind the pile of animal skins, rummage through my bothering bits. The smell of all that's gone before flows out from between my old clothes, the glider. But I persist, burrow deep into the small pocket at the side, find my little lead soldier and work my way back to my spot by the entrance. I run my fingers over the outline of his uniform, his rifle. What adventures we've had from that very first night when he tested out my tiny parachute! He's the one who got me this far. But he's been idle long enough, he needs to get back to work again. This time he's going to destroy the Sagittars. Gathering up a pile of stones from the ground around me, I shore them up into a circle and there's his own little dug-out to hide behind.

While he's planning his attack, I start with the soil at my feet, pour some water on it from the gourd by the fire, mix it up until it's nice and squidgy but not too squidgy so I can roll it into balls or flatten it like cakes. Then it's time to put shape on a head, long roly-poly pieces for the arms, scroll marks on the body, a spear on its helmet and I have made my first Sagittar. I start on the next one and the next and the next. Then I line them up to the side of the cave's entrance and let the sun bake them. General Yacobe will be ready for them by the time they harden.

I'm putting the finishing touches to some weapons for the general when I see Malfas coming up the hill, his catch for the day over his arm. He's not usually back before the others.

'What have you got there?' he says as he cleans his bloody knife on the side of his sleeve.

'It's just something Father gave me. General Yacobe. Ready to attack the Sagittars.'

He hunkers down beside me.

'Let me see.' He turns it back and over in the big palm of his hand. 'Well I'll be … I haven't seen one of those in such a long time.'

Then he sees the clay army.

'My son used to make things like that.'

'Koben?'

'Yes.'

'Does he not make them any more?'

'No,' he says, the quietest he has ever spoken to me. 'He's dead.'

'From the virus, like Mother and Seelah?'

'No,' he says more fiercely this time.

He goes quiet again and I hold my breath.

'Killed, with his mother. One of the buildings that the Sagittars had built for us to live in collapsed. They were buried underneath. It took days to clear out the rubble, to find their bodies.'

I remember Father telling us about that when it happened. Seven people killed, three of them children.

He stops and turns General Yacobe around in his hand.

'The Sagittars had called me in to the work station that evening to deal with some problems they were having with their Lexicon systems. One of them had crashed and they needed to back up all the sensitive data. It was while I was away from home that it happened. The building, toppling down. In the blink of an eye they were – gone.'

I don't know what to say. He's lost family just like us. It hurts all sorts of people, even tough men like him.

'Is that why you left, came here?

'Well … the Sagittars, they wanted to get rid of me after that. I knew too much. I had come across their plans about the Islands.'

'And?'

'Saw how they weren't full of viruses at all. That was the story they put out so no-one would come here. Saw their plans to build a sky machine. They knew about the gold. If they got their hands on it there would be no knowing what awful things they would do. But they won't get away with this. I'll find it, go back; get the indigents to rise up with me. We will defeat them. Then my wife and my son will not be forgotten.'

'What was he like?'

'He was … ah, it … what does it matter now?'

Then he takes up one of my Sagittars. 'Who's this?'

'One of the hoodies.'

Wham! A head rolls onto the ground.

'And this?'

'A burly,'

Phht. Gone too.

In seconds, the leader and his henchmen are all crushed into the ground.

Then Malfas stretches across and undoes the rope around my ankle. 'I don't think you need this any more.'

My leg feels funny without the binding. I shuffle around at first, trying to get used to it, go right out beyond the cave with no hold on me, then back in again. I don't know what to do with myself, my leg missing it, like it's the middle of summer and I'm missing winter. But not for long.

CHAPTER 13

'Time we check out the raft, start moving on. If you say it's on Colmen, then it's time to find the gold. Come!'

Malfas hurries us down the path, through spikers and stingers which spring back against us if we're not careful. But I'm ready for them and they won't scrape or sting me like that again. Along the path through the narrow pass, under the goat ledge where they still bleat down at us, over rocks, along a path that I have no memory of, until we come to the edge of the trees. He pulls back a canopy of green vines.

There is his raft of blackened tree trunks lashed together with pedal-pod wire. It has a little einkorn straw shelter at one end to keep the sailor from the worst of the weather. The sail that was lashed to the mast is in tatters, only scraps of fabric are left clinging to the wood.

'You need a new sail,' Esper says. 'Otherwise we'll just be going round in circles and end up going nowhere.'

'How do we make a sail, clever boy?'

'Some ripstop from the paraglider in Starn's stuff-sack at the –'

'You're not getting that,' I shout at him. 'We'll need it to get us back home.'

All that time spent making it and now they want to tear it up. Not going to happen.

'It's the only way if you want to get to the gold, bring all the treasure back. A raft with a sail is the best option.'

I hate to admit it; he's probably right, but …

Sucking in his beard, Malfas rushes back to the cave, with us charging after him, trying to catch up. He's out of breath by the time he gets to the hill before the cave, so I see my chance and overtake him. I have to get to it before he does.

'You can't cut it up.'

He laughs, grabs me just before I get to the cave-mouth, pushes me out of the way. My sack that survived cloud suck and zanderhags is waiting for him in the dark hole of the cavern. He pulls out the paraglider. Holds it up like a trophy.

'Come on,' Esper says. 'This is perfect for a rough square sail.' He unfurls it and, as he does, he shouts: 'Hey, what's this?'

The map falls to the ground. I jump forward to retrieve it. A big foot comes out and pounds my hand. The force sets up a rumble on the floor below us until it feels like everything is going to crash in on us.

'OWWW!'

'Ah-ah!' Malfas pulls it from under my fingers. 'The map.'

'Must have fallen –'

'What?' Malfas roars again. 'You snitchy-snitch. Lying to me like that, when you had it all the time. I've a good mind to throw you to Veltor.'

He hands the map to Esper. Even though he has told me about his son, it is still my brother that he turns to. I've broken his trust.

'Tell me what it says,' he demands of Esper.

So he can't read cursive. Just like the Sagittars. He may not be one but he's as good as. Father says that they aren't fit to rule Gazillony Park, let alone our territory, they're such dizzards.

The paper is very flimsy because it got so wet in the sea, but Esper can still make out the names of the islands.

Galyon

Vasuri

Colmen

and, further on,

Mannioc and Serpens.

'We need to get to Vasuri first, then Colmen, which is to the south of there,' my brother says.

'We could do with something to guide us, show us what direction to go in. A bearing dial, that's what we need,' Malfas says. 'I saw a design of one on Omicron.'

'Let me help,' Esper says.

So they set to work, at the front of the cave, while I am sent to pluck the birds for supper. I'm out in the cold again. It's a horrible job, pulling those beautiful flight feathers from creatures that have evolved over millions of years.

Veltor watches Esper watching Malfas, as he starts to

shape a circle of wood with one of the flint axes he found in the cave. Every so often he passes it to Esper, who whittles away with it, curls of wood piling up at his feet while he works.

'You need to make notches all along the edge like this,' Malfas tells him.

How I'd love to do that, to be working alongside him! I cut the head off the bird, pull out its guts as if it was Malfas.

One of the notches points south.

'Now the pointer. That way it can set our course. If, as you say, we need to go south; the bearing dial will do that for us.'

Esper looks at the map and confirms that Malfas is right.

If Malfas got here on the raft, then maybe, with Esper's help, we can return on it. If sacrificing the paraglider is the only way, then I have to give in.

So we set about making the sail. Borrowing one of the sharp stones that Malfas uses for skinning animals, we tear the fabric as best we can. Then we head down to the beach where the raft is, plait some of the thinner vines on the trees to make a rope strong enough to lash it to the mast. Malfas secures the bearing dial to the front of the raft. Soon it's ready for off.

Next thing is our store of provisions. We spend the day gathering stonefruit, blackfruit and any of the red fruits that the birds eat and won't kill us. We check all of the cradlebirds and snares, gather and cook as many birds and animals as we can find and wrap them in cold leaves to keep them from hoppers and clingers. We trek back and forth from the well in the cleft, fill the animal bladders with fresh water, secure them under the straw shelter. Four extra are filled and strapped to the underside of the raft to keep us afloat. The raft is beginning to look very small, the platform already a tight squeeze before we even get onto it ourselves.

We fall, exhausted, into our corners. Sleep is overcrowded with pictures of skinned birds and blackfruit floating before my eyes.

'Time to go.'

Malfas stands at the mouth of the cave and looks at the morning opening up before us. Esper has only the clothes on his back. Malfas too. I pull out the stuff-sack and push in whatever bits and pieces there are of the leftover glider.

'Leave that here. No room on the raft.'

'But, but … for bringing back the treasure.'

'If we find the treasure, we'll find ways of bringing it back.'

It's no good arguing. The sack falls off my shoulders onto the ground. A great longing comes over me then and I think of Orchard Territory. What if Father comes looking for us? How will he know we have ever been here? I stuff a small piece of fabric into a hole in the wall, enough sticking out so it looks like a little flag, put General Yacobe in beside it. Then, lifting a piece of charcoal from the fire, I scribble on the smoky surface below it:

FATHER. ON WAY TO COLMEN. HOME SOON. WITH TREASURE.

The three of us make our way to the beach, Veltor hot on our heels. Malfas and I start to pull the raft towards the water, while Esper talks to the wolf about where we're going.

'Veltor can't come,' Malfas warns Esper. 'There's no room. Not enough food to feed him.'

'I'm not going without him – and you two cannot manage without me,' my brother challenges him.

But Malfas isn't buying it.

'Fine. You stay behind with him. There'll be more food for me and your brother.'

'No! He has to come,' I plead. 'To help you use the bearing dial, to get us there.'

Esper looks at the sea, then turns around to view the forest, while Malfas is already moving the raft onto the water.

'You know you can't stay,' I shout at my brother, afraid of what he's thinking. 'You're the only one I've got. Please.'

He crouches down, puts his arms around the animal and whispers something to him, as he touches the medal around his own neck. Then he hurries to the raft and climbs in.

'Stay!' Malfas shouts back at the animal, jumps onto the raft and pushes off with the paddle. Veltor sits on the shore, turns his head to the sky, his ears pinned back, and starts to howl, his long knife teeth pushing the howl from his throat. The sound echoes all over the island. The rocks throw it back to us, *YOOOWL*, so that it sounds like there is a pack of wolves surrounding us.

'I'm not leaving him,' Esper says, but before he can jump

back off the raft, Malfas puts out his big strong hand and stops him.

'No! Paddle!'

We do as we're told but haven't made much progress when we hear the splash. All we see is the snout and the ears as he thrashes through the water towards us.

'Good wolf,' Esper says. 'I knew you wouldn't leave me.' He pulls him up onto the raft. The animal shakes himself, wetting us all over.

Malfas tries to push him off. The animal turns and snaps at him. Malfas draws back his hand, about to hit him on the snout. Veltor growls.

'He stays and you have to give him your rations,' Malfas warns Esper.

'Not a problem.'

Laughing with delight, my brother rubs the animal's ears and the animal licks his face over and over and over.

We start paddling again. Malfas checks the bearing dial to make sure that we are going in the right direction. The sea is calm, the sun warms our faces and, apart from the paddles swishing the water, there is very little other sound. A slight breeze barely ripples the sea as we make it round the sheltered side of the island, past the cliffs where the birds fly in and out of their nests. Wings flap above our heads, squawking and skirling. Soon we are leaving Galyon behind, moving out into the open sea, and our cave home becomes a dark spot behind us.

The breeze is now no more than a gentle puff. We move over the mirror of water, very slowly. Two of us keep the paddles going at any one time while the other rests. It's a tight squeeze with all of us on board. Veltor sits up like a Vigilant searching the horizon for any of those pirates that Father told us about, but there is nothing.

We share out the fruit first, some water, Malfas poring over the map to see what it tells him.

'Five islands altogether,' he says, counting them on his fingers. 'And this, what is this part?' He points at the riddle.

I read it aloud for him. 'This is what I told you about when I arrived. The treasure, see: that's the treasure.'

He seems satisfied, moving his finger along the words as if they would deliver the gold there and then.

The sea stretches out before us. We seem to be paddling for hours. Bobbing up and down on the swell. Tides are running in our favour and, apart from the odd spray, it's pleasant on the raft. Now we cannot see land in any direction, as the waves lap around us and the sun starts to go down. Esper feeds Veltor half his ration, and if wolves can smile, this one does at my brother. I try to move in close to Esper but he's having none of it. He pushes me and I go sliding over the side.

I come to the surface coughing and spluttering, grab onto him and pull him in on top of me. Veltor is quick after him, and soon we are splashing and playing in the water.

Esper pushes my head under.

Keeping a good eye out for zanderhags, I see all sorts of fish scooting by but none of those monsters. My brother's legs are there too, kicking away. Grabbing him by the ankle, I pull him with me. We stay down until our chests are bursting, come up for air; shake the water off our faces. Push one another down again, then up to the surface. He laughs, I laugh, water running off our hair, down our noses. We are laughing. Together. He looks like his old self, his face bright and clear, Veltor swimming in around our legs.

'Come on, Malfas. There's no zanderhags.'

Malfas pulls off the Godwins' earth-suit, his body all old and white and wrinkly, but he jumps straight in and soaks us all over. The raft is bobbing up and down beside us.

'Hey, guys. Look.'

Treading water, we turn to where Esper is pointing. A tiny but amazing green spot gleams where the last ray of the sun still hovers on the skyline. It disappears and returns again for a few seconds, flashing and reflashing. We continue to tread water as we watch it on the horizon. Until it's shut off as if by a tiny switch and is gone.

'That was alpha – a green ray,' Esper says to me, and for a minute he seems like the old Esper again, relaxed and happy, excited by something new and telling me about it.

'You remember, then?'

'Remember what?' he says, swimming away from me and starting to splash Veltor. I think his memory is coming back but for some reason he doesn't want to let on.

'Let's get out.'

My skin is wrinkled and goosebumped from the cold and as I begin to pull myself out, there is a sound that stops me. It's very quiet at first but then as it gets closer it sounds like birds honking. It gets closer and closer, the noise becoming as unbearable as the siren back on Orchard, and before we know it birds flap and wheel towards us. We watch, astounded, as they all land in one fell swoop on the raft and fill every inch of it. Soon we cannot see any wood at all. Only white wings with black tips that are as wide as our paddles are long. Bright-pink legs. Their squawking is horrendous; it's so loud my eardrums nearly split.

'Marleogs.'

A bird that my E-pistle told me was wiped out before the Ash has now taken over our little space in the sea.

'Shoo, shoo,' we shout, flapping our arms in the hope that we will frighten them away, but they don't budge.

Veltor swims to the edge of the raft, opens his jaws, but they flap their wings, beat him on the snout and across his eyes until he falls back into the water. They start pecking at our supplies, pulling out the fruit and stamping on it with their big bright-pink feet. We cannot stop them. Their honking is more than we can bear.

Each time we try to hang onto the edge of the raft a huge spear-sharp yellow beak reaches out, pecks and pecks at us, tries to pull out our fingernails. There is nothing for it but to dive under the raft where the water skins are tied to it. We cling to the ropes that have lashed the wood together with just enough space for us to breathe while the birds gobble and honk above our heads.

It's very cold. The birds go quiet for a little while, nothing but the odd flap or half a honk. Esper's arm is around Veltor so he won't fall away. Left here much longer, we'll die of the cold or zanderhags. Or both. We hang on.

Just before the sun finally disappears, there is movement about us and below. The current is getting stronger. Steps waddle on the boards. There is a great whirring and, as if on one collective wing, they rise up, honking and flapping as they arrow into the air. Off to roost somewhere else. One by one we drag ourselves back onto the raft, all mess of feathers and guano everywhere. It's so smelly, it's worse than Malfas on a bad day.

He starts to pull his earth-suit on. They must have been dancing on it because it's covered in the mess, and they've destroyed any of our rations that they didn't manage to eat. The leaves have been shredded by their beaks and blobs of purple and red stain the platform. The smell of bird is so strong I feel sick, hungry and tired and ready to fall over the edge of the world.

We clear away as much of their mess as we can, flicking the guano off the side of the raft with the long flight feathers they have left in their wake. As soon as Malfas puts his earth-suit back on, he plops into the water so he can wash the smell of bird off it. We rifle through the bits of food but there is very little we can salvage. There is a handful of nuts that we rinse in the water too and we eat what we can of them.

Suddenly Malfas hauls himself back onto the raft. Water drips down from him as he grabs one of the paddles and searches around frantically.

'Where's the other one?' he shouts.

Esper pulls it from the straw shelter at the edge of the raft and waves it in the air.

'Why?' we both ask.

'Quick,' he orders us. 'Hold onto it tightly. The water's changed. It's getting choppy. Secure the shelter.'

But there isn't time for that. The raft lifts and falls on the waves. Before I know it, a line of frothing spume whips across the surface. Then the surf begins to boil, bursting upon us.

'Back-paddle! Back-paddle!' Malfas shouts.

We all grab our paddles and start into reverse. Waves are being whipped off the huge rocks and some monster is driving us into a place where the rising waters strike and wallop into each other.

The sea whirlpools all around us as we try to back-paddle with every last bit of energy. We just seem to be swirling around in the one place, being pushed towards the bank of a standing wave, spinning, spinning, wheeling like a whirligig.

Water explodes under us, bubbling up in huge mountains of surf, spiralling, spiralling, as we are whipped in all directions. We are being slurped down into the black eye of the vortex, our paddles useless against the force, the raft being jounced and shaken upon a sound like the ground rumbling when Malfas pounded the floor of the cave. There is nothing for us to do but hang on.

'You can do it, you can do it,' a tiny voice says in the back of my mind, as we hold ourselves back.

'Veltor!' Esper screams.

In the last of the light, we watch the wolf being sucked into the maelstrom.

CHAPTER 14

Weathered faces stare down at us as we lie sprawled across one another on our raft, which has crashed onto the rocks. Malfas's big leg pins my arms to the boards, Esper's scream still echoing in my ears as he tried to catch Veltor before he was slurped down into the big black hole. Whatever Malfas managed to do, he saved us from going over the edge, making us paddle like that, making us hold on for dear life. So he's not all bad; there's a good man in there too. Maybe he was thinking of his son when he gave us the orders to hang on.

'Are you injured?' one of the islanders asks. Malfas shifts his leg, giving me some breathing space.

'We're fine,' I say, 'just a bit bruised.'

The islanders have long hair, tied back in ponytails, their clothes made of a very coarse fabric roughly sewn together. I've seen them on old footage on E-pistle, trousers and shirts, fabric like the ancients used to wear back then. They put out their hands and pull us onto solid ground.

'We'll go straight to Corvus, so,' another of the men said.

The island is stonier than Galyon, the beach full of huge boulders that we have to weave in and out between. There's none of the creamy sand of the beach where I first landed. From the rocks, men are casting long lines into the sea.

We walk towards green hills that roll down to the water's edge, head towards some trees. The islanders flip-flop ahead of us in their rope sandals. The smell is different here; I don't know why. And voices. I hear voices far off.

The sun is flooding our way as they steer us along the path. Shadows move in and out through the branches. Where there is a break in the woods, water thunders in cascades down the hill, the river broadening out to push back the forest as we go deeper into the valley.

We hear them before we see them: the women drumming the water. Standing in the swollen river as we walk by, they beat the wet surface as if it's a giant liquid drum. The sound swirls all around us. They're washing their clothes, beating them on the stones, making music as they work. They wring out the clothes, spread them on the rocks and come towards us.

'Hi, Davys, hi, Jep, Rubin,' they call out. 'Who've you got there? Thought you told Lin you were gone fishing?'

'Well, we've caught us a real catch today.'

It looks like the trees have been cleared and now fields of neat rows of green sway in the breeze. Further on a woman is pulling a rope out of the ground and a container appears out of the hole. Liquid splashes from it as she turns to fall into step with us, while more greetings are called out. Further on a group of people go about their work, gathering something from the green patch of field around them, straw hats on their heads. They stop when they see us, leave down their tools and start moving in our direction. Soon we have a cavalcade of people marching behind us, calling and chatting to us, all asking so many questions that we don't know who to answer. Davys puts his hand up, tells them to leave it until we get to Corvus. That they will hear everything then.

Somewhere in the distance there is a sound. Like a howling.

I look at Esper. He hears it too. Could it be? Ah, no. He went down. Way down.

We pass a field of blue. Esper is talking to one of the women, Netty; she tells him it's flax and they plan to harvest it, spin it into fabric for their clothes. Mounds of stones are dotted all along the sides of the river and glint in the daylight. Malfas is talking to Rubin as if he has known him all his life.

The land opens up into a clearing and there is a circle of houses on stilts, roughly shaped huts made from big logs with roofs of woven leaves. There are women cooking in front of the huts. Pots boil and bubble, and whatever it is it smells good.

'Dad, Dad.'

Two children stop their running in and out of the huts and come laughing and shouting towards their fathers. Something inside me flops. More children join the procession behind us until we come to a humungous tree that stretches up into the sky.

A rope ladder dangles from it. Looking up I see a house built into its crown. It's bigger than all the rest. Davys climbs up first with Malfas behind him; Esper follows. I do as I'm told and climb up too. I step into the big wooden room. My first sighting of the man they call Corvus is of a person much older than Father and Malfas, smaller, rounder, sitting on a wooden block at the back of the tree-house. His long hair is white. There are dogs sitting at his feet. How did they get up here? The walls are lined with boxes and crates, wheels and cans. He has a small box on the ground beside him. He sits there with his eyes closed, while, shuffling and pushing, everyone piles their way in behind us, trying to squeeze in between the walls made of tree bark, until the house is heaving.

'So who have we here?'

'Castaways. Washed up on Isleta Point.'

'I am Corvus, leader of the island. You are welcome to Vasuri.'

We repeat our names to him, where we've come from, the catastrophe in the whirlpool. Corvus's eyes are dark as blackfruit, steely sharp.

'So you've come from the Territories. Which one?'

'Orchard.'

'People still live there?'

We look at one another. Why wouldn't they?

'We thought you were all dead. That there was no-one else left. How have you managed to survive?'

So I tell him what we left behind, the grey world of the Sagittars, the rationing of heating and food.

He just nods his head as if it all makes sense to him.

Malfas says nothing. His stare fills the space as the

rings on the leader's fingers glint in the light that pours in through the openings in the bark walls. One little boy, with bouncing curls, sticks out his tongue at me. I make one of Seelah's funny faces.

'Colome,' his mother says. 'Behave yourself.'

Giggling, he burrows into her shoulder while all around us so many are clamouring to ask us questions.

'Is Orchard still producing the best fruit in the land?'

'There are only apples; most of the other trees were destroyed by the Ash. But they're trying to bring them back. They have set up a plant nursery.'

'That is so sad. And what are the Sagittars doing about it?'

We tell them.

'Still? After all this time? Has no-one been able to overthrow them?' I think of Father and his wish to see the military rulers knocked off their perches. 'So what brought you here? How did you get here?'

All the people lean in towards us to see what we will say.

'We came on a raft.'

'No planes, no boats, even?'

'Not since before the Ash.'

'No wonder the skies have been so quiet. So they're all gone,' Corvus says and a wistful look comes into his eyes.

'What route did you take?'

Kneeling down before him, I pick up a twig and draw circles in the dust and fire ash to show them where we landed on Galyon, the leaving on the raft; the vortex that we escaped from.

'STOP!'

CHAPTER 15

His voice goes through me and I drop the twig. What have I done wrong now? Corvus picks up a ball and throws it at me.

'Catch,' he shouts.

Instinct makes me stretch and catch it easily in the palm of my hand. Another man throws a round piece of wood. I catch that too. Esper and Malfas look as perplexed as I am. The girl sitting beside the leader then throws a piece of fruit. It comes fast and hard at me above my head; but, jumping up, I grab it.

It's like some kind of test and I'm the only contestant. All I can do is play along with them in the hope that I will prove myself, so, running the length of the tree-house, I grab whatever objects they throw at me. The thin balsa walls vibrate with the movement of the crowd and me running back and forth as if I was in Gazillony Park. A big cheer bounces off the roof each time I catch something. It makes me feel good, like I'm a champ. Then Corvus throws something down real low, nearly out of my reach. I hold my breath as it comes spinning towards me. I stretch out my left hand and, *THUMP*, it bounces into the bowl of my fist.

The biggest cheer of all goes up.

Corvus reaches out and clasps my fingers covered in dirt. The wrong hand. My left one. Oh, no – can I never get away from it bringing me trouble? But joy lights up his weathered face.

'You have proven yourself; you have used the hand of the Vasuri. You're a Vasuri, a left-handed one.'

The girl beside him gives me a big smile, and he holds up my arm as if it were a trophy. It's only then I realise he has his staff in his left hand too.

Malfas turns to Esper and whispers something in his ear. My brother shakes his head but Malfas immediately picks up a stick in his left hand and waves it around.

'You too?' the leader asks.

'Yes,' Malfas lies, shaking the stick even more vigorously.

I bite my tongue. Everyone claps and looks pleased, especially the girl. Esper's head is bent, as if he's looking for something he's lost in the thin film of dust on the wooden floor.

Corvus beckons me to sit to the left of him. 'I had a dream the other night,' he says. 'I saw a green ray at the foot of the sun and it spelled out that there would be new Vasuri coming to help us. And now you turn up. It's a sign. I always believed this would happen. More people will continue to come, and before long we will have enough strength of numbers to go back and storm the Territories.'

His words give me goosebumps. Was that the same green ray Esper saw just before those terrible marleogs got us?

'So you'll stay,' Corvus continues, rubbing the head of one of the black-and-white dogs beside him, 'and help us with the cause?'

'Of course,' Malfas says, but I can read his mind. All he sees is gold, gold, gold. He is staring at the glistening ring on the leader's finger.

'I don't plan to stay, do you?' I whisper to my brother. But he doesn't answer.

Instead he turns to talk to a boy younger than us sitting nearby. The boy has a creature cradled in his arms. Taking the animal, he drapes it around my brother's shoulders. That's enough to bring the light back into Esper's face. The animal starts nibbling at my brother's hair until he dissolves into laughter and we are back to where we were before all this happened. It looks so much like Seelah's Snowy, though its back is stripy and it has white paws.

Malfas is still waving the stick and talking loudly, saying that he wants to help the cause and that he knows lots of confidential stuff about the Sagittars. Corvus is all ears.

Women are coming up the ladder with baskets of food, serving us like we were bigwigs. We eat, juice running down our chins. This is a coaxiorum day the likes of which we have never known in our lives. Soon my belly is as full as Opson Stores, only better. The heat of the fire, the long days on the sea and the rich food soon make my eyes begin to droop.

But Malfas is asking Corvus how they got this far so I sit up straight and put my sleep on hold.

'I'll tell you that shortly, but first it's time for everyone to go back to work.' Then he turns towards the crowd. 'Off you go now. You'll get the chance to see our guests in the morning.'

They thank us again for coming, say goodbye and, one by one, they head down the ladder steps. Rubin puts one of the dogs into a straw basket and carries it down the ladder with him.

The girl beside Corvus doesn't budge, though.

'Leone, go with your mother,' Corvus commands.

'No.'

I'm surprised at her defiance. You wouldn't catch either of us talking to one of our leaders like that.

'How many times do I have to tell you to do as you're told?'

'And how many times, Pops, have you told me and my brothers that the only way to learn is by experience? If I'm ever going to help the cause I have to hear the story again, the story that you haven't told in such a long time.'

Corvus has no answer to that.

'Well, OK so, just this once,' he says at last, knowing that she has won. 'But if you interrupt me too many times then it's the ladder.' And he points to the opening through which the others left.

She grins across at us, plonks down beside the remaining dog and puts her arms around him. She's about the same age as me, her hair is cut very short and, for a girl, her hands are big and strong, like she is used to hard work. I think of Seelah's hands, how small they were, how delicate.

'Start,' she says straight away, ignoring her father's earlier order, 'from the beginning, about how you left some years before the Ash and all ...'

So Corvus starts by telling us how the Sagittars were beginning to persecute those who were left-handed. Left-handers were shunned, because they were believed to be dangerous and evil. They couldn't get jobs, which meant they were condemned to poverty and hunger.

Corvus had seen that the situation was becoming dangerous, so he rounded up anyone he knew that used the 'wrong' hand. They met in old basements or underground passageways, and they worked out a plan. They would leave the Territories and make for the Islands. Eight families left Orchard, including eleven children. Nine more children had been born since the families had arrived on Vasuri.

'I was born here,' Leone says proudly, swinging her legs back and forth. 'But before that they came in three big boats and –'

'Are you telling the story or am I?' her father says, not too unkindly. Then he tells how they sailed across the water and lists all the things they brought with them: as much food as possible, a seed bank of crops and vegetables, some medicines, tools, knives. Enough to get them started. They brought dogs, some cats; there wasn't enough room for bigger animals. But they could manage with what they caught in the sea. They cleared the land, planted it. Already they were working on ways to make fabric from the flax growing in the fields.

'They're the blue flowers that we saw along the way? The ones that Netty told us about? Aren't they?'

Leone is in before her father can get to answer my question. 'That's them. Mother knows a lot about making cloth and wants to teach me but I'd much prefer to be working on the treasure with Pops.'

'Treasure?' Malfas is in like a shot.

'Stop calling it that,' Leone's father says.

'Well, I think that's what it is.'

'I've told you. It's nothing of the sort, but it will be of value to us at some point.' Her father turns away from her and continues to tell us the Vasuri story. 'We were a few years here when the ground started to rumble. We watched the plumes, the clouds of smoke and ash in the sky beyond us,' he said. 'We thought it would cover us too, that we would be destroyed; luckily, the prevailing winds around the islands were our saviour. The Jet Stream carried the ash away from us. But it did bring on flooding.'

Esper, who has been quiet most of the time, wants to know if that is why they have tree-houses.

'Clever boy, that is exactly right. The flooding hasn't been so bad in the last seven years but we like living high above the ground now. We already had to clear the trees to make land for planting. So it was a good thing to be able to use the trunks for our houses. Nothing gets wasted here.'

I think of home.

'We always thought others would follow,' Corvus says then, 'that they would want to get out, just like us.'

So I explain to him that the Sagittars filled the waterways with zanderhags and told everyone that the Islands are full of disease.

Corvus goes quiet for a few minutes. Then he says, 'As you can see, they have been lying to you. There is no sickness here. Did no-one else try to get out?'

'Not that we know of, but –'

'I had friends, you know; they'd said they would come, that they would follow on when they had their boat repaired. Bring others with them. But all these years and nothing. I wonder have you any news of them? Tymon. Would you know him?'

I tell him that Father has a friend of that name.

'And the Godwins? Did you know them? They had planned to come too.'

I look at Malfas but he's too busy still looking at the leader's ring to react. I don't want to tell what I know, so I just shake my head.

Corvus shows us the things they brought with them, lined up on the shelves around him: their tools, their boxes of seeds. Every year they harvest seeds from what they grow to make sure they have enough for the following planting. A big chronometer sits on the shelf, doing nothing.

'It stopped working soon after we arrived and none of us could get it moving again.' He laughs. 'Maybe one of you bright boys can fix it?'

'Not me,' Esper says, 'but our father could.'

Why did he say that? Is his memory …? Could it …?

'Tell me again why he didn't come with you.'

'Are those binoculars?' I reply far too quickly, in the hope of distracting him. I'm pointing to a black case that sits on the shelf beside the chronometer.

Leone goes to the shelf and takes the binoculars down, hands them to her father. He shows us how to use them. Esper and I stand at the door of the tree-house, taking turns to focus on the world beyond us. We're able to see far across the sea. I think I can pick out Galyon and maybe that's Colmen over there. The other two I can't find. Corvus says that, most likely, Mannioc and Serpens were covered in ash.

Then Malfas takes the binoculars from me and searches this way and that around the island. What he's looking for I don't know but he must have found something because he turns to the leader.

'We'll stay and help the cause,' he says, his eyes staring at the chain around the leader's neck, greedy with longing.

'I want to stay as well,' my brother says.

I turn to him. 'But we can't,' I hiss.

'Why not? They have everything here that we need.'

'But, but – the treasure. Bringing it back to Father.'

'Well, what if it's here?' and he just turns away from me while Malfas is promising the leader all kinds of things he will do for the islanders.

'He's as bad as the Sagittars,' I want to shout out. 'Don't believe him.' But I don't have the nerve.

'It's time you were shown your sleeping place.' Corvus

stands and we follow him and Leone as they move towards the ladder.

Down the rope we go, to be greeted again by the people who are gathering up their tools for the day. We step across the stony path of the island, followed by the children, who clap and cheer us.

Malfas bows and waves as if he is monarch of all he surveys. Some young men take their drums and the drumming soon fills the island. *DA-DUM, DA-DUM.* We step up, halfway to the sky, into the house that will be ours. Soft bivis are scattered here and there.

'You must be tired,' Corvus says, 'so sleep.' He waves his hand towards the soft pillows of leaves, the warm rugs. 'Tomorrow we will get you to help us with the work. We need all the hands we can get.'

The moon comes up over the trees and shines in the door of the house as we bivi down. There is only the sound of insects click-clacking in a hidden pocket somewhere outside the tree.

I have no memory of falling asleep and don't wake until a blast of sun shines through the window and the birds start calling from the branches.

We have no sooner moved our heads but breakfast appears. More fruit and bread and something so sweet that it tingles on my tongue and explodes stars into my mouth.

A head appears at the top of the ladder. It's Leone.

'Time for work,' she calls.

The day has opened up bright and cheerful as we step down from the ladder. They walk us along a different path this time, where the trees arch above us across the walkway, shading us from the day until they thin out and we see ahead of us the whole village gathered. The children come following as soon as they see us. Malfas starts waving his hands around again, acting the bigwig.

We are directed to a row of logs in front of a stone platform that leads into an underground shaft. They have a pulley that goes into the earth and a big metal container is hauled up and emptied out. Mounds of stone are piled in front of the hole in the ground and piles of soil are dumped in other mounds all around too.

'We were clearing the ground when we discovered the metal-bearing stone sticking out of the soil,' another man, called Mack, tells us. He's a big strong man, his arms like thick ropes as he pulls away on the machine. 'There's loads of it underground, and when we have enough we will search out new islands that we can trade with. Then we can build up our own army against the Sagittars. Soon we will start transferring this stuff into the boats. We will show you those later.'

'Where are the boats kept?'

'Beyond Isleta Point. Where you landed.'

Sunshine glints on the stones and a seam of burnished rock shimmers in the light. For a moment it's almost too bright for us to see anything around us.

I see what Malfas sees. Gold?

He is so excited he can hardly contain himself. He mucks

in and we all take it in turns to empty the buckets as they are pulled out.

We work all day, side by side with three other boys, not much older than us but twice as strong. It takes my brother and me all our strength to lift a bucket that they manage easily on their own.

'Do you not want to go home?' I whisper to my brother. 'Me and you back with Father as soon as we get the treasure.'

But he's more interested in the collection of creepy-crawlies that are gathering around our feet.

'Look,' he says. 'See how their bodies curl up when they feel in danger.'

I know that feeling myself.

When it comes time for a break, the islanders waste no time bringing out the food, loaded upon platters of bark. Leone comes and sits with us, curious about our lives, what it's like in Orchard, especially what it's like in Academy. They don't have anything like E-pistles here, so she wants to hear all about them.

The sun's rays continue to burnish the stone, gilding all around it.

Malfas asks Leone, 'Is this the treasure you were talking about?'

She has just bitten into a slab of bread and her reply comes out all crumby but it's the answer Malfas wants to hear.

'Yes, but it's not really g–'

'Leone,' her father calls, 'I need you to go back to fetch more water.'

'Looks like we don't need to hunt any further,' Malfas whispers as Leone skips back to her father. 'The gold is right here in front of our noses.'

'But – but – Corvus said it wasn't treasure. And my map?'

'They're stupid. They don't know what they have. And who is to say your map isn't wrong?' Malfas sneers.

'No. It was definitely Colmen.'

'Maybe that was done to fool people, stupid people. But not me.' He looks greedily at the wall of rock with the gilded seam, as if all the food around him isn't enough, as if he needs more than all the Vasuri can feed him.

CHAPTER 16

Somewhere a night bird hoots, a dog howls, but it's the *creak*, *creak* of the bark-wood floor that awakes me. The moon shines through the opening and along the space between our bivis. Esper is curled up in a ball, fast asleep, but there's no Malfas.

I pull on my trousers as quietly as I can and make my way down the rope steps. A shadow ahead of me slouches like a big animal towards his mission. Not a sound from him, no mutterings to himself as he covers the ground. Step by quiet step, I weave in and out of the shadows, making sure he doesn't see me. The moon, his lantern, lights his way as he lurches under the archway that leads to the shaft. Leaves rustle, the ground sucks up the sound of our steps.

Crouching in the dark of the trees, I creep as quietly as is possible, trip up and fall heavily against the hard trunk of one of them. Righting myself, I hold my breath, but he mustn't have heard because he makes his way towards the mound of stone without turning back.

Mack, who is on night duty, has fallen asleep, his head nodding on his chest. Malfas creeps up behind him and, without mercy, crashes his head with a big rock. Mack's groan fills the still night as he slumps to the ground. By the time I get closer, Malfas has started hacking off lumps of the precious metal and shoving them into the bag he has taken from his shoulder. The night air is shattered by a voice that booms from behind us.

'HALT!'

Before I can even open my mouth, strong arms shoot from behind and pin me to the ground. More workers rush to Malfas. In the blink of a govey's eye we are overcome. My hands are locked behind my back, tied. Malfas fights with all his might but he's no match for them.

What has he done?

Rubin grabs me and bundles me under his arm like a log, while the others restrain Malfas, who is kicking and roaring. I feel ashamed. Even though I didn't do the damage, I may as well have. They have treated us so kindly and I have broken my father's wish that we never do harm to person or thing. At least Esper is spared. He would never be caught up in something like this. Maybe he'll explain to them that I wouldn't damage others' property. But then he doesn't even know I'm his brother, does he?

The moon dances in and out through the clouds as we're hauled back along the path where we had walked just a shut-eye earlier. Then they veer in another direction, towards the mountains, while I, the dizzard, look out into the dark night from under Rubin's arm to see Malfas being dragged behind me.

They arrive at a mound of earth and I am eye to eye with a heavy wooden gate in the side of it. One of them pulls it open; the others catch us and fling us into the hole. My mouth hits the ground and the taste of blood fills my mouth. Then the gate slams shut, the bolt shoots home and something is rolled in front of it.

We are prisoners.

Malfas attacks the bars and shakes and shakes them but there isn't a budge. He rams his shoulder against the gate. 'AAAAHHH!' he roars as if his shout will bring the barrier down. He tries again. Not even the tiniest budge.

If the cave in Galyon was dark then this is humungous dark. It's smelly too, so smelly I can barely breathe. Animals might have lived here once, for the scent is musk and earthy. There is also another smell that reminds me of something else, but I can't put my finger on it.

I curl up in a ball in the corner. Sleep has gone for a long walk somewhere and it's not going to come back tonight.

As spikes of dawn peek through the bars of the gate, I hear footsteps come along the path. At last. My shoulders come down from my ears. That wasn't too long. We'll be out before a Sagittar can say *psittacosis*.

But it's not what I hoped. The gate is dragged open and Esper is thrown in right on top of us.

'What's going on?' he snarls at me. 'I was fast asleep and they just came and pulled me out of bivi. They hauled me down the steps, shouting at me that we were spies for the Sagittars.'

'Malfas took some gold.'

'Well, I don't care what he took, no-one's going to haul me around like that. Hey, wait a minute, did you say gold? What gold?'

'From the mounds of stone.'

'That's not gold.'

'What do you mean?' Malfas says, pulling a piece from his pocket. 'Smart boy with no memory, what is it, so?'

'It's iron pyrite: fool's gold. You find it in seams along with lead galena. That's what they've been mining from the earth.'

'Fool's gold? There's no such thing.'

'There is so. I overheard Jep talking to Corvus about it. They've already checked it out by heating it. Gold doesn't change colour when you heat it, but iron pyrite does, and anyway I remember once reading it on my eeee …'

'… pistle,' I finish for him. A shiver runs through my body. He almost remembered.

'So the gold isn't here. The map was right.' I look at Malfas. He should have believed me.

'Nothing for it but to get to Colmen.'

'What are the chances of that?'

'Nil. Nada.'

'OUT!'

The gate is pulled open and light floods the pit. They grab Esper and me under their arms, then drag Malfas out between them. They march us to the spot where only the day before we were the best thing since vita-shakes.

Corvus stands in front of us and says, 'We trusted you and you betrayed us. We treated you as part of our family, gave you our food, our beds and this is how you've repaid us. Damaging our property, taking it as your own. Pretending you were Vasuri, left-handed, when you were just like those snakes we left all those years ago. We have our own laws here. The Vasuri deal with things their own way.'

'But –' I start.

'No-one said you could speak. Once a Sagittar. Always a Sagittar.'

That's the worst thing they could call me and there's no point in trying to get them to see that we're not, and that I didn't want any of this. All the other times I thought I might die, up in the clouds or under the sea, I always was able to fight it. Now this power is taken from me, because we broke these people's trust.

Malfas is shouting and roaring at them: 'The Sagittars will come and kill you.'

They laugh back at him. 'There is no-one but the Vasuri. You should not have come here. We told you our story and we trusted you. Take them back to the pit. Then bring the dogs.'

To the sound of the slammed gate, my brother and I sit huddled together waiting. Malfas is still roaring and thumping the gate.

'Wait until the Sagittars come. They'll destroy you.'

He doesn't accept that his words haven't a hope of putting fear into the Vasuri.

'I'm sorry,' I turn to my brother, 'for all the times I

fought with you, called you dizzard. You are my family, no matter what. All the things I said back then when you told Craster about the book. I shouldn't have said them. I was just cross with you, jealous of you. If this is the last time we're together then I want us to be brothers before we go. As Father says we only have each other so we have –'

'– to stick together.' He leans across, punches my shoulder like he used to.

'Hey, you remember.'

'I, I, I … don't know, my head feels all funny. It must have got a terrible wallop again when I fell from the raft.' He hits the side of it as if there's something loose. 'Phew! This place smells like a souterrain.'

'What's a souterrain?'

'An underground passageway. And if there is as much flooding as they say there is, then it's my guess that there could be underground rivers.' He sniffs. 'If I'm right – and I'm always right – then there's another way out.'

That's my brother.

He starts moving along the dirt walls, tapping as he goes, checking for water seepage. It all sounds the same to me but this time I have to believe him. A little trickle runs from one of the spots where he stops. *Tap. Tap. Tap.* It sounds different. A hollowness that echoes back to us from the rap of his knuckles. Has he found the way?

'Malfas, I need you to help me. NOW!'

We all get down on our knees without a complaint and take turns clawing away the soil, flicking it back with our hands as if we were animals making a burrow.

Scrape, scrape, scrape.

CHAPTER 17

'Shh. What's that?'

'Sounds like the dogs barking at the moon. It'll stop any minute now.'

'Don't you think it's getting louder?' Fear brings a shiver to my voice.

We all stop and listen. I'm right. The baying gets sharper. Nearer. And worse, there's more than one.

What are they going to do? Set the dogs down the tunnel after us? We won't have a chance.

'Quick, quick! Let's keep working. It's our only hope.'

Malfas doesn't waste a second. There's a madness to his strength as his shovel-hands dig into the earth and fling piles of it behind him, shoring up the gateway, creating a barricade against our attackers. Esper better be right about there being a way out through here. Otherwise we are completely trapped.

'Quicker!' Malfas shouts. 'The dogs are getting louder.' Fear makes us work even harder, as we all pull whatever strength we have out of our arms. One last effort, one gigantic surge, and we claw back the dirt, push until, YES! The wall comes tumbling down. The air released from the earth stinks even worse than the pit itself, but there's no time to be choosy and the howling drives our bodies through, coughing as we breathe in the foulness.

Disgusting.

With great difficulty, Malfas gets his shoulders through the tunnel. He's huffing and puffing as he inches slowly behind us, making very little progress.

We can hear the groans as the gate opens back at the entrance. The mound of earth we've thrown up with our digging just has to hold them back, it has to. If it doesn't we're meat-sap.

Frustrated barking travels down the corridors and fills the chamber, mixing with our fear. Angry shouts follow behind as the job of clearing our barricade begins for the Vasuri. We inch into the darkness, coughing and spluttering, trying to catch our breath. Malfas is grunting like a wild animal as he forces his body through the corridors that the old river has left behind but he's making progress by the sound of it.

My lungs are about to explode any minute, but then my elbows seem to have a little more room as the corridor opens out a bit and Malfas is able to make more headway too. We continue to crawl through the dark, dirt falling on our heads and our legs freezing from the water, afraid to speak to one another, until Esper begins to cough. He's unable to catch his breath. This is what always worried Father about the ash when he would get an attack. That's why he always had a mask at hand for him.

No masks here.

Something catches my throat too, and water begins to stream from my eyes.

'What's wrong with –' Malfas begins, but his words are strangled in his throat as a fit of coughing overtakes him. Soon none of us can catch our breath. Like a snarling dragon, the smoke comes billowing down along the tunnel and we are all spluttering and gasping.

I'm terrified of fire and smoke ever since we saw pictures of the way the volcanoes exploded into the sky, and magma and lava destroyed all around us. Now the fear wells up inside me at the thought of being surrounded by smoke while the weight of the earth presses in on top of us. All I can do is stretch out my hand to touch Esper's foot. He puts his hand back and grasps mine tightly.

'Come on,' he says, 'we can do it.'

We crawl along the tunnel, the stony clay tearing my knees to ribbons.

'Think it forks into two here,' Esper says. 'This way.'

Trusting him, I follow. So does the smoke that keeps us gasping and coughing, without any let-up.

'Oww.'

'What's the matter?'

'This fork. It's a dead end.'

'How do you know?'

'Just hit my head off the wall.'

'You and your smart ideas. You were wrong.' I cry out into the hollow. The darkness echoes all around us. 'There's no way out and we're going to suffocate. I don't know why we believed you in the first place.'

'Don't give up now. We just chose the wrong fork. If it's not one, it's the other. Malfas, back up, out of here. Take the other path.'

Luckily, he has to save his breath, which stops him from roaring at Esper, and he puffs and splutters as he reverses his bulk back the way we came.

I force myself to do the same, then my brother and, gagging, we head back. The smoke's getting worse. If we can't find our way out we'll end up as nothing more than a pile of bones.

We elbow our way along through the other fork of tunnel. We could be going round in circles and getting nowhere for all I know.

My breathing becomes a little easier. 'Does anyone feel it? There must be fresh air coming in somewhere,' I say as, little by little, my lungs begin to ease out. The dank smell of the tunnel is being replaced by something more up-on-landish.

A blast of air rushes in as Malfas reaches the opening. 'I'm out!'

'Hurry, just another few minutes and we'll be out of here, too,' Esper claims.

Our knees shuffle towards the freshness. With one collective heroic effort we push ourselves forward and fall out into the night full of clean air. We lie there gasping. I look up at the sky. I used to think it was dark. Now I see little pinpricks of light. It's like daylight compared to the tunnel.

'This entrance is on the other side of the hill. They won't

pick up our scent for a few minutes. But we need to be well ahead of them before that.'

Taking in quick gulps of air, we hurry through the night grass, gathering speed as our lungs recover.

In no time the dogs have picked up the scent and change their cry from one of frustration to one of chase. We run as fast as our legs can carry us. We crash and tumble against the stones and hummocks that come up against us at every turn. The other two are making good headway, but I'm lagging far behind.

Youwl. Youwl. Youwl.

Esper turns to check on me. 'Did you hear that? It's not the dogs. It sounds like … It couldn't be, could it?'

He hardly has the words out of his mouth when he runs straight into a rock and, before I can grab him, he's lying on the ground, moaning. Rushing towards him, I try to lift him up.

'Don't. I think I've broken something.'

'Come on, I'll help you.'

'No, you'll be caught. Go on without me.'

'Lost you once, not going to let that happen again. Come on, up we go.'

With his arm around my neck, we hobble in the direction of the beach, the baying of the dogs getting nearer and nearer. We scramble over the stones and lay him on the raft, which Malfas has pulled from the rocks. Then we push off, paddling with the strength of a hundred people, as the first dog comes charging towards us and bounds straight into the water.

Malfas is about to take the paddle and bring it down on its head when Esper cries and grabs it from him. 'No, it's Veltor.'

The wolf comes whipping through the water, jumps up on the raft on top of Esper and starts licking him all over.

'Where did you come from?' Esper demands.

Malfas grabs the paddle back from him and lashes out at the other dogs as they try to make headway through the waves. With a great thud, he wallops the first head, then the second, the third.

His aim is true and sharp; he keeps whacking the water as the dogs whimper, and one by one they fall into the rolling sea. Malfas tries to push Veltor back in too, but the wolf snaps at him, and he quickly drags his hand away. Esper is in charge of the animal now, and Veltor settles down beside my brother.

I can hear the Vasuri as they in turn come thrashing towards us. They have picked up rocks from the beach, put them in their slings and now they send them zinging through the air. Malfas and I paddle for all our worth as the stones rain down on us without mercy. One grazes my shoulder, another Esper's arm. Malfas takes the worst of the blows, right on the side of his head; and, for all his strength, it's too much for him. His big frame slowly slumps on the raft right beside Veltor.

CHAPTER 18

There's blood running down Malfas's cheek. The paddle slips from his grip and sinks, and his pain-filled groans fill the space around us. Esper's in trouble too. He already damaged his ankle, and now he's holding his arm, his face is gashed and his hand is red with blood. He's lying up against Veltor, who hasn't moved since he got on the raft.

I've no choice; it's all up to me now. My left hand does me proud. It takes on the other paddle and lashes through the water until the Vasuri give up. Their last stone plops into the waves just out of range of us.

One small problem, though: I don't know where I'm going; don't even know which way the tide is running. We could be heading back to the Vasuri and where would we be then? Maybe they'll come after us in their boats. But no! They won't want to waste the fuel on us.

And now there's nothing but wreckage all around me: the bearing dial is broken, the map is missing, the tattered sail has been ripped off by the whirlpool, the little straw shelter has collapsed.

Dragging on all my strength, I pull us through the dark

sea, nothing in the sky but the same blackness. I rest for a little while, lie there looking up. Soon my eyes get used to the night with its tiny pinpricks of stars that have come to live with us again. I wish I could read the sky, find out where Gemini is – the twins' constellation. Mother used to tell us how at the beginning of time one of those twins was immortal, the other mortal; they lived between the sky and the earth, and when one died in a big Greek war, the other was inconsolable and a god called Zeus made them eternal in the night sky. She said, if we looked to the northeast of Orion, we could find them. But we never had skies clear enough to see them. How can I pick them out now? I don't even know where Orion is.

'Aghh. What happened?'

My brother is awake before me, holding the side of his face. It's swollen where one of the rocks had hit home. Veltor is licking the dried blood off it. The sun comes up over the horizon and paints the morning sky a glorious pink. Malfas is still in a ball on the edge of the raft, no movement from him; no life in him at all.

'Should we check if he's still alive?' I suggest.

'Well, if he isn't, then we'll just slip him overboard,' says Esper. 'The raft would be much lighter without him. And who'd ever miss him!'

'We can't do that. It would be wrong.' All this time we've spent with him, I don't want to harm him. He hasn't harmed us. I think of the stories he told me about his son.

Malfas was a father too. 'Remember, he saved you.'

'He wasn't the one who saved me.'

'Who, then?' I ask.

'Veltor,' says my brother.

'Don't be daft.'

'With all the buzzing going on in my brain, I just can't think straight. All the wires are tangled up, and the signals are going in all sorts of directions.' He slaps the side of his head again, as if to try and clear it, then stretches across and puts his ear to Malfas's chest. 'He's still breathing. Pity.'

How cruel he has become! I've never seen such meanness in my brother before. He wouldn't have said that if it were an animal. Then he continues as if he had read my mind, like a twin.

'I don't like when someone is nasty to animals, Veltor especially.' I suppose that explains it. 'My head really hurts. And my ankle.'

He pulls up one of his socks; the ankle has swollen to three times its size. One of his cheeks is red and angry, the eye blue–black. He looks like one of those indigents from the grid that the Sagittars were violent to when they found them on the street.

'Get that into the seawater,' I tell him. 'It'll bring the swelling down. And wash the blood off your face.'

He grabs his injured leg, forces it over the edge of the raft and sinks it below the surface. 'That's better.' Then he splashes his face with the seawater. 'There's all this noise storm-whipping up in my head. I can't bear it. As if different wires are trying to find a way to transmit. And I'm thirsty, so thirsty.'

So am I, my tongue and lips dry and parched. All this water around us and not a drop to drink. It's so tempting, but we can't touch that salt water or it would make us really sick.

'Condensation – there should be some around here. Somewhere. It was cold enough last night for it.'

Was it? I don't know what he's talking about. Then I remember our last science class, distilling water, how it condensed on a cold surface.

'See that piece of ripstop over there?'

He points to a rag of sail fabric that is bunched and shaped like a bowl beside the collapsed shelter.

I stretch across to check it, but there is no water in the little trough. All the times we read about sailors who were able to collect enough dew in tiny wells of fabric to keep themselves alive, but there isn't any for us. Any bits of fabric are so torn or shredded that they're no good as vessels.

We plop into the water to keep our bodies as cool as possible, to protect us from the scalding sun. Dip our heads under. What I wouldn't give for the tiniest drink!

Back on the raft, I can feel my skin burning on my arms, the top of my head, my nose. I crouch behind Malfas, his unconscious bulk offering little respite from the scorching sun and we just

drift drift drift drift

drift drift drift drift

drift drift drift drift

CHAPTER 19

A voice, somewhere across the great big ocean.

'Yoohoo! Yoohoo! Answer if you can hear me!'

'We hear you, we hear you,' we both croak together.

With a splash of oars, a boat comes bouncing across the waves and pulls up beside us.

Then – the sweetest thing – a small dark woman throws a rope to us.

'Grab!' she roars.

Stretching out, I catch it, hold it tightly, as she begins to reel us towards her.

'You look like you've been in the wars,' she says after taking a glance at our cracked lips, our bruises.

Even sweeter than throwing us the rope, she stretches down and, from the bottom of the boat, finds a flask, passes it to me. Pulling off the cap with whatever strength I have, I take a slug of its soft, fragrant liquid, gulp it down. It's so lovely, it's like a light has gone on inside me. Esper grabs it from me and I hear it gurgle down his throat, and his face begins to lighten.

I rub a few drops on Malfas's lips. He doesn't respond. Whether he's dead or alive is anyone's guess. Veltor is not forgotten; Esper pours some down his throat too.

Our rescuer continues to pull us through the water, and there is the sight of silver wings in the sky. Land birds. I watch them fly and flap above us. There is the sight of a landing wall and, as we get closer, more boats bob and swing against the brick wall. She guides us through them, while men and women wave down at us. They look enormous as our tiny craft is steered towards them.

Hands stretch out to help us up out of water and onto land. There's a feeling of coming home that gives me the usual collywobbles in my belly. Boatwoman helps us up the steps. Veltor stays close to my brother, protecting him.

'We'll see to your father,' the woman says, and I don't have the energy to correct her.

Malfas is still unconscious. With great difficulty they heave him off the raft and move him as carefully as they can to a stone bench between piles of nets and wooden crates. They tell us to sit beside him until they have him comfortable enough to move.

'Easy,' one of them says to us when we gulp down the sweet drink in the flask. 'Too much too soon could make you sick.'

We sip slowly, waiting, as people scurry around us attending to Malfas.

'So you've come.'

The morning sun burns through the clouds and I have to shade my eyes from the glow that's coming from the tall, regal woman who stands before us. A miniature version of herself clutches her hand beside her. All those overpowering events have me seeing things. For a minute I could swear it's Mother and Seelah. As I rub my eyes, the picture clears, and it's not them. This woman is taller and thinner, though her face is soft, her smile warm.

'We have waited a long time for this day that Tartesah foretold.'

'You knew Great-aunt Tartesah? But, but –'

'Hush! That is for later. You were very lucky that Lili came across you, or you would, most certainly, have succumbed to the waves or the sun. I am Irina, Queen of Colmen, and this is my daughter, Helena.'

Helena gives us a little wave. She is about Seelah's age, but her hair is dark and she has a bouncing, healthy look about her that my sister never had.

'Altair.' The queen's voice rings across the air.

An old man hobbles towards her. His hair is very thin, silver, and his body is shrunken, one shoulder curled towards his cheek, whose skin is wrinkled as a withered gunnera leaf.

'Yes, Majesty.'

'Let's attend to their wounds. Their father looks like he needs serious attention. We will bring him to the central enclosure.'

'He is not our fa–' I start, but she doesn't hear me, too

busy giving orders to Altair and the other workers, who come with a stretcher to lift Malfas onto it. The imprint of the rock is still on the left side of his face. The blood has dried into a dark red crust.

'And you, young man –'

Irina turns to Esper, who's limping along, still holding his head.

'I'm fine. My brother will help me.'

My heart leaps. The wire circuits must be clearing themselves. He's coming back to me.

Leaning against my shoulder, he draws himself up the green road, following the stretcher-bearers, the wolf keeping very close to him. Happy heads of flower blossom are everywhere and the air is heavy with scent and the hum of insects.

'Even the butterflies are welcoming you,' Helena says, pointing to a beautiful insect with wings of red and blue.

So *this* is what Father meant when he used to talk about 'butterflies in my stomach'. I'd seen some bugs on Galyon and Vasuri, but I never thought they could be as colourful as this. Other stripy insects seem to be flying ahead of us, and every so often they stop and do a little wiggle dance.

'They're bees, aren't they?' I ask Helena.

'Of course. Welcoming you. Tartesah would have told the colony a long time ago all about you coming.'

I get the collywobbles again. Bees – Aunt Tartesah. All the work we have to do in Orchard because this little stripy insect has been killed off by the ash. Here it is flitting from flower to shining flower and nothing to bother it. How can they know all about us coming here? What sort of powers had Aunt Tartesah?

The trees sway back and forth in the breeze and up through them the blue eye of the sky winks back at us.

'Look, the enclosure, we're nearly there now,' Irina says by way of comfort to Malfas, though there is still no response from him.

Hexagons! Rows and rows of six-sided buildings frame the land in front of us. Some are single storey, others have one built on top of the other.

'Look, Esper! They're the same shape as the symbols on your amulet.'

Esper puts his hands to his throat, where he still wears Father's prize. There were drawings like them in the book too, but I hadn't taken much notice then, as I was too busy looking at the map. On the top of each building is a panel, facing the sun. Gathering the energy from its rays.

'Look! They're just like pollinators, from Orchard,' Esper shouts. As I turn to where he's pointing, men in white suits cross our path ahead of us and disappear into the woods. Before I can say they must be bee-keepers, he looks at me and asks, 'Why did I say that?'

'You must be getting your memory back.' Something inside me starts to settle. 'Does that mean …?'

'… we're brothers? Suppose. So stop annoying me by asking me all the time.'

Altair makes his feeble way towards us. 'You look so much like her. The same –'

'Chin?'

'Nose?'

We both chip in at once, and everyone laughs. So they do recognise us. Father and Mother weren't just making it up, telling us fakers.

'We have waited a long time for you.'

His own eyes turn misty and he rubs them as if a bit of ash has blown into them. He seems kind. He organises his helpers to carry Malfas into the central hexagonal building ahead of us. I help Esper in after them. Irina and her daughter are already there before us with two medics.

'These are Tartesah's boys,' she says to the waiting nurses.

They smile at us. 'At last.'

Then they bring Malfas to a small room at the end of the building and close the door.

'Let's see to you while they attend to your father. He's worse than we thought. We will have to do a lot of work on him. But don't you worry; we will look after you until he recovers.'

'He's not –'

'No,' she says kindly, 'he's not going to die.' She has misunderstood me again.

'Bring your pet in here beside you. He seems to be the only one that doesn't need our attention. Now, how about a nice drink and some salve for those injuries. Altair!'

'Yes, Majesty.'

Altair staggers off, comes back with a large brown jar and hands it to her. She dips her fingers in and spreads the amber salve on our blisters and on our cuts. It cools the anger in them straight away. But better than that: the old man passes a brimming cup of liquid to each of us. It's the same liquid that Lili gave us and it fills up my cells straight away with a similar flash of energy that zooms down my legs and up again, then across my shoulders and down my arms. I see the transformation in my brother too. He's beginning to look his old self again and walks up and down the floor with barely a limp. Veltor is slurping away from the bowl put down in front of him.

'After you've had a good rest, we will show you the house.'

'Where Tartesah lived?'

'Yes. Of course.'

The treasure. Finally. We've waited so long for this that I'm all ready to go and head towards the door.

'No,' she says as sternly as Mother would. 'Your bodies need to recover from your ordeal. Altair will sit with you until you have had a good rest.'

There's no use protesting; she makes us lie down at once.

I only wake for a drink to wet my parched throat, passed to me by the old man, before I crash back into the arms of sleep. All day and evening and into the slumber of night, my brother and I sleep on and on and on as if there was no tomorrow.

CHAPTER 20

We wake: all bright-eyed and govey-tailed, ready to tackle the day. My brother sits up in the bed beside me, his old self. Whatever special drink Altair gave us, it has washed all the pains and aches out of me and I'm ready to go again. As soon as the old man sees us with our eyes open, he turns on his skinny heel and he's off to get us some food.

'Do you remember now what happened after we were sucked up into the clouds?' I ask my brother.

'It's all a bit shaky still, a bit like the screen on Omicron before it's logged on fully. The one thing I do remember, though, is the cold. I remember that most of all, and falling.'

'How could anyone forget that?' I say. 'It was the worst freezeday ever.'

'I can't remember what went on between that and being catapulted out of the glider, into the sea. I blacked out after that. When I woke up I was being dragged through the trees and being licked all over.'

'Veltor?'

'Yes, he saved me. Something funny happened there

between us. The most peculiar thing ever. I'll never forget it.' His voice wobbles a little. 'The crazy thing is that it was as if all the reading I had done about animals suddenly came to life.' He touches the charm on the cord around his neck. 'Remember the night Father talked to us about him and Mother living here and how Tartesah had a gift? I think, whatever it was, it saved me then. The animal saved me. He'll always save me.'

'What do you mean by that?'

'I don't know, just that he's my best friend.'

Jealousy floods my heart and I try to kick it away by saying: 'Will you ever want to come back to Orchard, to Father?'

'Only if we can bring Veltor with us.'

Lili comes in then with a tray full of coaxiorums for us: soothing drinks, sweet cakes and bars that are alpha. We feast on all we want in the cosiness of the room until the queen comes to check on us.

'Your father still hasn't woken up but he is no worse, so we'll leave him in peace for the morning.'

This time I don't even try to put her right because she says, 'Tell me when you feel up to it and we'll show you around. I have a real treat for you.'

We don't have to be asked twice. We're up and throwing water on our faces, pulling on our boots and out the door.

'Hey, boys.' Irina laughs. 'I wouldn't like to see you if you were in a hurry.'

We start with the first hexagonal house. Even the door has glass shaped into hexagons and she pushes it open and calls in: 'Helena, I'm going to show the boys around, if you want to come with us.'

Helena appears and beams at us. As we walk by the rows of other hexagonal homes, boys and girls are playing in their gardens or helping to pick big bunches of brightly coloured flowers.

'Do they not have to go to Academy?'

'It's Mellifera time: the time when we celebrate all the goodness the bees. They're getting tired now, having been working all the summer, gathering nectar, pollen, making wax. They have provided us with all of this.' She waves towards the trees and the flowers. 'Without them we would not have survived, we'd have died away. Soon it will be time for them to overwinter. But before they do that we have our very special festival. Tartesah started it, so it will be great to have you here this year as our honoured guests. Later, we will go to the learning centre and start preparing. That's the building over there.'

She points out a series of hexagons at the end of the enclosure.

We continue to walk, past the learning centre, the provision stores, Helena pointing them out to us as we go. We laugh at the sign that says

QUIET PLEASE. BEES AT WORK.

'That's where all the hives are,' Irina says. 'Down that path through the trees, a quiet place where they can do their special tasks. I'll show you that later. But first, Tartesah's house.'

She guides us to another opening in the trees; we follow

her in and out through windy paths, through leaves and moss and bright red puffballs, the river keeping pace alongside us. We wander up and over wooden bridges that are only a step wide but take us clear of the rivulets that funnel their way across our path. Everything is alive and new. We come to a small gate that swings open like it's welcoming us back. It all feels so at-homeish.

'Let's go inside.' The queen opens the green door, worn with age, flaking off the years of cobwebs and leaves that have gathered around its edge. 'No-one has been here since she died.'

As soon as I step inside, I start to shiver; it gathers in my belly first, spreads down my spine and through my knees into the earth. My knees are wobbly, my hands are shaking.

'Do you feel it?'

My brother just nods his head. His hands are shaking too. It creeps up my back; all my bones turn to jelly. My head gets all woozy. It's a scent that is familiar and something more than that, something that was captured in the Book of Gold and got opened up in Seelah's room the day we discovered it.

'So this is it. Tartesah's house.'

I look around at the tiny space only big enough for one person. Two small hexagonal windows look out onto the river. The water sounds its way all along the side of it where it rises and then falls, its white foam gathering circles in the trapped rocks. There is just a table and a chair and a small bivi with a bundle of blankets. Strange objects lie around. I pick one up. A smoker, Helena calls it. Her mother shows me the decapping knife, the hive tool, all the equipment used for looking after the bees.

Veltor creeps in under the table, which is still piled high with wooden frames that have the same writing on them as if our great-grand-aunt had just gone out for a walk. The dust of all those years sits on her writing, that cursive, that I first saw when I discovered the book. I wonder if it's being displayed in Biblion now? Or did the Sagittars just destroy it? No-one will know what it says unless someone smarter than us was able to decipher the strange script.

'She saw things,' Irina tells us. 'Things only special people saw. She predicted it, you know, the volcanoes erupting. She warned the Colmenites not to leave the island or they wouldn't survive. That if they stayed this side of the Ash to mind the bees, they would not be wiped out.'

I'm trying to take it all in. *Start small*, I hear Mother whisper in my ear.

'All of this she wrote down and put in the book she left for you. She gave it to your father and mother before they left the island. She didn't want them to go, but they were young and didn't hear what she was trying to tell them. All they saw were the better opportunities there were for them on the mainland. She told them to keep the book for you when you were born. Then the Ash came. That Colmen was spared such destruction is a miracle.'

'How did she know that we would come, that we would be twins?'

'She knew things no-one else ever dreamed of. She could see how the bees would be wiped out. She got those who stayed behind never to leave them and so it has become our life's work. She put it in the Book of Gold for you.'

'But we couldn't read it, understand any of it. Except for the map, it was like no language we ever saw.'

'She had to do that so it didn't fall into the wrong hands. Did you not know what she was doing?'

'No.'

'Mirror writing, of course.'

Dizzard! There before my nose and I never thought. If it was any simpler it would have jumped up and bitten me. Like my best friend, Leonardo da Vinci, who got us here in the first place – he wrote backwards too.

'It would have been so simple if I had understood that.'

'Maybe you wouldn't have bothered coming here if you had read the whole story.'

'So she knew we would come?'

'The wise part of her did. She was an extraordinary human being.'

'Where is she buried?'

'We don't know. When she got very ill she went out one morning for a long walk and never came back. It was like she was just spirited away. But enough of that. Let's go and check out the bees. I think her old bee-keeping suits are in this cupboard, somewhere.'

Irina steadies me while I step into the white protective suit, and I zip myself up. It's so big for me it's like I'm being swallowed in one big gulp. I roll up the sleeves and the trouser cuffs just like Father did that day long ago in the pollination station. I put my nose to the sleeve just to get the scent of Tartesah. That's enough to get the wobblies doing somersaults in my belly. Over and over again.

Then she helps Esper into another suit. We follow the queen through the trees, down a slope past the sign that still says '*QUIET PLEASE*' and work our way along. There's a great hum as we get towards the hives. It gets louder and louder. Then we see them, their brightly painted houses on stilts lined up in semi-circles in the secret enclosure; bees busy, buzzy, all around us, flying in and out their little front doors.

The Apiary.

'Look at their pollen baskets.' Irina points to a bee crawling in through the opening of one hive. At the back of the insect's legs, two bright yellow sacs are attached.

'So that's what they look like. It must take them ages to gather all that,' I say, remembering the sweepings that the Defender of the Seed swept off my suit when we were at the pollination station.

'Bees visit three hundred flowers a trip, so they're bound to collect a lot of pollen on the way.'

She takes the crown off one of the hives, lifts out a frame. It's packed, crawling, with bees, climbing all over one another. She picks up one of them, bigger than the rest, to show us.

'Are you not afraid it will sting you?'

'This one's a drone. He has no sting.'

She hands it to me.

I don't let fear stop me as the brown and yellow creature crawls all over my gauntlet, checking me out. She shows us the nectar shiny in the cells; the cells that were once covered with wax before a new bee emerged, are now empty. As Irina explains it to us, I realise all we learned about pollination was nothing compared to what it is like in the real life of a hive.

CHAPTER 21

Before she can show us any more, Altair comes floundering down the path towards us with as much energy as his frail body can muster.

'Your father is acting very strange.' The old man has to lean against the tree to catch his breath. 'He's woken up and is shouting something about gold; trashing the room and saying that he will do damage if we don't tell him where it is.'

'He's not our father.'

'What do you mean, not your father?' asks Irina.

So I tell her how Malfas was already on Galyon when we landed on it. He was after the same thing as us. 'The gold.' I speak in almost a whisper.

'What gold?'

'The gold on Colmen.'

'There's no gold here.'

'But Tartesah's book said … the riddle …' Esper recites the four lines for her, remembering every broken word.

'Ah! I see now.' Irina laughs. 'Come with me; I'll show you the treasure.'

I knew it. It wasn't a made-up story at all. At last, we'll

get to see what we came for. The riddle said it would save us. As soon as we tell Irina how we need it to save Father and Orchard Territory, surely they will share it with us. For Tartesah's sake. Then we'll be able to head back home to Father.

She turns again towards the hives.

'So this is what you've come for.' She takes the lid off one hive, lifts out a board laden with honey.

'Here it is: a frame of gold. Liquid gold. This is the treasure Tartesah means.'

'Oh.'

I look around for gold bars, nuggets, coins even, but there's nothing, nada, just the bees crawling all over her hands without her flinching. The same disappointment is on my brother's face. We came all the way for this, nearly losing him in the cloud suck, being attacked by zanderhags, being pulled down a whirlpool and all the time it was a few hives. How can we go back to Father with nothing to show for the trouble we've caused him? If Malfas is right and Father is in the detention unit, he'll have failed the Fitness to Father programme and we'll be signed into Nanny Care. All this for nothing.

Irina breaks off a piece of the 'gold' honeycomb and hands it to each of us. I bite into it. So sweet, its softness melts into my mouth. The golden liquid runs down our fingers but it won't be wasted. Every precious drop we lick from each of our fingers and then we ask for more.

From somewhere, Mother's words come right back to me, when I was hanging on the glider and thinking I was dead. What was it she said? Faithfulness to getting the job done, not leaving Father on his own. There's no other way. We have to go back, even empty-handed we have to go. We could bring him some honey, though. He will have forgotten how it tasted.

'There's another surprise I have for you before we go back to check on your fa– no, your friend. Helena, will you please run back and tell the medics that I am on my way. Altair needs to catch his breath.'

Helena does as she's told and skips off in the direction of the centre. When Altair has recovered enough we head back, keeping in time with his step so he doesn't fall behind. We arrive at another little hexagon almost hidden by the trees. Irina lifts a latch and we walk inside. It's dark, smells like Tartesah's house. There is someone sitting in a chair by the window.

'You'll never guess who I've brought to see you, Sibby.'

Sibby? Wasn't she the nurse who looked after Mother?

An old woman looks up from where she is. She's more like a bundle of clothes with just a wizened face on top.

'I was hoping you would bring them. Come up right close so I can touch you.'

Irina whispers to us that the old woman cannot see.

Up beside her she is even older than I could ever imagine. Her skin is as crinkled as the broken ice on the pedal tracks at freeze-time. Her eyes look out at us all milky and sightless. We stand in front of her. She puts out her hand and touches our faces, one after the other. Of course she mentions the nose, the chin.

Her fingers are cold but not unkind.

'I looked after your mother when she was a child.'

'Yes, she told us.'

'I'm glad she didn't forget me.'

We're sitting each side of her, her gnarled fingers holding onto ours. She tells us the story in her own words. When Mother's parents were drowned, it was Sibby who minded her. She saw our mother grow.

'I will leave you for now,' Irina says. 'I'll be back for you when I've seen to the preparations.'

We sit with Sibby all afternoon, and she tells us about Mother growing up, her interest in the great world and how it spun. She smells of wax and sweetness. We are no longer alone.

Tears run down her cheeks when we tell her how Mother died.

'I always wanted her to stay, but she was in love with your father. The world was theirs for the taking. There was so little here for them to do. To have her two boys back here is more than I ever dreamed of. Though Tartesah was always convinced that you would come some day. And now here you are. Maybe you will take on her work, if you stay, that is.'

I don't tell her what I'm thinking.

We say goodbye, promising to come back the next day, and when Irina collects us we retrace our steps to the centre. Veltor picks up the scent of an animal and rushes off through the trees. As we skirt the place of the bees, birds scatter out of the branches, squawk up into the air, creating a terrible racket. The wolf must have frightened them. But no. I search the sky, and then I see it.

'Look!'

A ginormous red ball with something hanging from it moves across our line of vision. The sphere moves, ascends, then descends again and we shade our eyes to try and see what it is. Maybe it's a ball of ash that has caught up with us. It floats over the trees, its big red shape skimming across the sky. A basket hangs underneath it and, as it slowly descends, faces peer over the side. It's a balloon, a hot-air balloon! We all run to where it's falling, into the centre of the enclosure.

They've landed by the time we get there, jumping out of the basket, three, four, five of them. The first things I see are their helmets. They make my heart stop.

'Irina,' I hiss but she doesn't hear me. 'Irina, hide.' She moves towards a low wall in front of the enclosure.

I pull Esper behind the tree, my heart pounding.

The Sagittars have caught up with us. The last time I saw them I was running from them, Interim Winds howling, boys piling onto the pedal-pod. What will they do when they find out there is no treasure? My brother's body is shaking beside me. I'm no better and grab his arm to try and calm my own.

It's just like Malfas predicted. How they were planning all along to make a machine to get here. And they did just that with their balloon. Obviously it was a good design, for it carried five of them to this spot. They run from hut to hut now, brandishing their Tevlar guns, kicking in the doors, shouting at everyone to come out.

What will they think when they find out what the gold really is?

No-one appears, and then they do a terrible thing. They take a container of liquid from the basket and pour it on the first house, then throw a lighted taper into it. An explosion of flame bursts through the little house, the beautifully shaped window panes blown out. They do the same with the next one and the next one. Smoke is billowing through the roofs, covering all the air around us. We can just about see as they torch the central building.

'HELENA!' The scream from Irina is almost unbearable as she rushes towards the flaming hut where she had sent her daughter with a message for the medics.

Phtt. The sound of the Tevlar gun assaults the air.

Irina tumbles to the ground.

'Can you not call for Veltor?' I whisper to Esper.

'No,' he says. 'They'd hear me, shoot straight at us.'

Suddenly the bee-keepers come charging through the woods with nothing but their white overalls to defend themselves. Stun bullets come hailing towards them. *AAAHH.* One by one they fall. More bee-keepers take up where the others have collapsed. Another spray of bullets sends them toppling. The workers have given all they can, but without weapons they have no defence and the bullies know that. Father always said they were capable of the worst crimes.

Soon there is no-one left standing but Altair. We watch from our hiding place as he drags himself slowly forward.

'What do you want?' His breath is feeble, his speech barely audible.

'The gold.'

'There is no gold.'

'Don't play that game with me!'

I recognise that voice. It can't be – can it? Mortice? Craster and Tuan's father? The man who loved to tell jokes, to tell riddles. He's as bad as the others.

'The gold – or else,' our friends' father says before he lifts his gun and aims.

Altair starts chanting something.

'What are you saying, you stupid old man?'

Altair defies them and continues to chant aloud words that we don't understand.

Soon there is a long plume of dark buzzing wings heading towards the attackers. Sagittar howls of pain echo all over the clearing, as the swarm ups its attack. Stinging, stinging, stinging. The old man continues to chant as insects cover the clothes of the Sagittars like a buzzing blanket, even as Mortice pulls the trigger and Altair falls to the ground.

The invaders turn on their heels and run out of the central enclosure straight towards the cliffs, the bees in angry pursuit after them. We hear human cries of terror. Then silence.

Crawling along the ground under sheets of smoke we belly our way towards the injured. The aftermath of the battle is a sorry sight. All the white suits piled on top of one another on the ground. It will take hours for the stun toxin to wear off. We continue to crawl until we are sure it's safe to stand. We run towards the learning building. Enter it.

'Anyone there?' we call out.

One of the cupboard doors opens and Lili tumbles out with a clutch of children huddled behind her.

'We were just preparing the bee bread for tomorrow when we heard the shooting,' she says. 'So I bundled everyone behind the doors. What has happened?'

'Sagittar attack,' I explain. 'They came out of the sky. A balloon. Used their guns on Irina, Altair. They're gone now, though. The bees drove them away. It's safe to come out. But we need help with the injured. And Helena – she was in the medics' building. They torched that. We don't know if she's OK.'

'Don't worry. I'm sure she's fine. I'll send someone to check on her.'

As we all head outside, other adults and children come rushing out of buildings to see bodies everywhere, the smoke hanging in the air, the big balloon now deflated. All around, bundles of bees are dead on the ground beside us.

'It's what happens to them,' Lili explains. 'They sting; they die.' Lili is a strong woman and an organiser. She sets to straight away, ordering people around and getting things done. She half-lifts, half-carries the bodies to the central chamber of the school. She calls out the children's names. They all reply in small, frightened voices.

We make Irina as comfortable as possible until the stun serum wears off. One of the workers comes back and calls

Lili aside. Though they're whispering I can hear enough to make out that there is no sign of Helena. He promises he will go back again with more workers when the smoke clears, do another search.

Some of the boys and girls start crying when they see their parents in their white suits lying there so lifeless. Lili tells them that they are only asleep and will wake up soon. Altair is the easiest one to bring in, his body so light, his bones as hollow as a bird's.

'I think it was more than a stun-gun that got our faithful Altair.'

We wait up all night watching for the workers to recover from their attack.

'Father! Mother!' each child cries, as Lili lets them run towards a parent who is starting to sit up and rub the spot where the poison entered their flesh.

Dawn is breaking over the smoking hexagons when Irina wakes up. Her first words are: 'My daughter, did you get her out?'

We have no answer for her. She reads our silence and rushes out the door towards the blackened building before we can stop her. We follow, hot on her heels, towards the charred door. We pull at all the rubble but there is no sign of anyone. We come out coughing and spluttering and head towards the other hexagons, calling Helena's name.

A familiar mumbling coming from behind one of the beehive huts stops me.

'Shh. Listen.'

Only one human sounds like that. I've heard it over and

over again from the moment I hung upside down on a Galyon tree.

Malfas.

He lumbers out from behind the hut, a bag over his shoulder. He drops it down on the ground beside him, faces Irina. A small whimper comes from it.

'Gold – or I kill her.'

He opens the sack and, grabbing her by the waist, pulls the girl out, bundles her under his arm.

'Mama,' she cries, holding out her hands to her mother, but Malfas catches them and forces them behind her back.

'Mama!'

'Helena!'

We watch Malfas put his big hand around her neck. I've seen the way he has twisted birds' necks. Without thought or care.

'There is no gold,' the queen says. 'You are still ill. We will help you.'

'There is nothing wrong with me,' he roars, the rage of a hundred gigantiums bursting out of him. 'What do you take me for? A dizzard? The treasure. Give me the treasure or she's dead.'

Helena cries out again.

'He's not lying,' I whisper to Irina. 'We have to do something or he'll kill her.'

'But you saw for yourself.'

'Malfas,' I shout. 'It's not the kind of gold you think.'

'Don't!' he roars back at me.

Then Esper shouts, 'Veltor! Veltor! Where are you?'

But there is no sign of the wolf. He calls again, more loudly this time, frightening the birds out of their roosting places.

'Velt-oorr!'

Before I can say a word there is a rush through the trees, followed by the familiar animal sound as he bounds towards us. He comes to a stop between my brother and Malfas.

'Veltor, to heel!' my brother commands, and the animal slinks towards him.

'Come back here!' Malfas orders in return.

Veltor stops in his tracks and his huge yellow eyes stare at Malfas, whose arm is still lassoed around Helena. She is so quiet, I hope she is still breathing.

'Veltor, get him!' My brother screams and the animal stops for a second, confused. Esper shouts again. 'Do as I say, go for him!'

With that, the wolf goes straight for Malfas, jumps on him and knocks him to the ground. The wild man howls and drops Helena from under his arms. We hear the clunk as his head hits the ground. Esper sees his chance and runs forward. I follow. We grab Helena by a hand each and pull her out of danger, into the arms of her mother, who holds the child fiercely to her body.

CHAPTER 22

Mellifera Festival doesn't happen. There is little to celebrate. So many injured, Altair dead, his frailness sacrificed for the survival of the island, thousands of bees dead too. Three Sagittar bodies have washed up on the stones near the cliff, the other two probably devoured by sea monsters. Craster and Tuan will have to learn that news about their father before long.

Malfas is hanging between life and death. The cold punch of the ground has fractured his skull. He has lost too much blood to survive. Helena doesn't want to be anywhere near him, so they bring him deep into the woods to a small secluded hut. Guard workers watch him night and day. Irina goes every few hours to minister to his wounds.

'After all he's done, would you not just let him die?' Esper asks.

I know what he did to Helena was terrible but I think of him losing his family. I think of Father.

'He hasn't long left,' Irina says. 'I will make his last days as comfortable as possible.'

In between times, we go to Tartesah's house, curl up together in our great-aunt's bivi with all the covers, and cosy into it. We take turns looking at the wooden tablets piled up on the table. They have been covered with a layer of wax. Letters have been scribed on each one, using some sharp instrument. All this makes me realise how much was destroyed in our land before we were born.

We head back to Sibby's to hear more of her stories about the island, about the world of Tartesah as she had recorded it: the bees spinning honey out of the combs, the people collecting the wax, the royal jelly for the queen. When she mentions how they added honey to almonds to make marzipan, I remember. *Marzipan*. 'That was the last thing Mother craved before she died.'

She takes a few moments, trying to find the words, her eyes focusing on nothing.

'Your mother meant so much to me. She was the nearest thing to family I ever had. What if you both stay here and I will mind you? I don't want to lose you now, after all these years. And when I'm gone, you will have others to look after you. Learn all you can here so you can take it back with you when you have grown up.'

For all the wonderful things they have on Colmen, I know we don't belong here.

'Our lives are back in Orchard,' I tell her. 'It was where we were brought up. Where we knew our mother, our sister.'

I talk about Father, how hard he has to work, how sometimes he has no work at all. The more I think, the more I miss even vita-shakes and malt bars, our E-pistles, going to Academy. But most of all I miss Father. I imagine him logging onto CWC and saying with all the care he has for us, 'How are my two precious boys today?'

'But we could come back and bring him with us. Now that we know you are here. We could bring him on a visit and he can see how things haven't changed since he and Mother left.'

'I'd like that,' Sibby says, her voice falling into sleep. Soon she is snoring quietly.

CHAPTER 23

'So you're sure you want to go back?' Irina asks as we cosy up in Tartesah's house, Helena sitting close beside her.

'Yes!' we both say together.

'But you've no-one to go back to. If your father is in the detention unit is there even a home for you?'

I look at Esper. 'That's why we need to go back. To get him out.'

'I know you're brave – but two boys against those thugs?'

'There are good men still there: Coach Danarius, Professor Kalmus. They'll help us, and when we were on Vasuri, Corvus told us about a group that were still working to bring the Sagittars down. Father's friend Tymon was one of them. He could even have got Father out by now.'

'There won't be much of a reception for you if you're going back without gold, without any treasure.'

My eyes wander all around Tartesah's room, picking out her books and bee-keeping equipment; so much knowledge just sitting there.

Of course. The honey.

I see it now.

It's pure gold.

'But we could still do that. Imagine if … I mean … what if we could bring back some bees? Get them to pollinate the apple trees, the plants in the nursery. We could grow new fruits, get Labspace to start new varieties. Then our trip wouldn't have been in vain.'

'Hmm,' Irina says. 'It's not as simple as that. A colony needs a lot of care …'

'But if anyone can teach us, it's you,' I say, my excitement mounting. 'We'd listen to everything you'd tell us; learn every single thing about them. We'd be good bee-keepers. Honest. Wouldn't we Esper?'

'We'd be alpha,' he says.

'It's what Tartesah wanted, isn't it? Otherwise her leaving the book to Father would be in vain,' I continue.

'What can I say to that, other than she would be very proud of you. So let's see what you're made of. Pull on your bee-suits. It's time for lesson one.'

She talks all the way to the Apiary, about the queen, her drones, her workers, about making sure they have enough stores in the winter, about keeping them warm. We watch the bee-keepers checking for any damage to the hives that might let in predators or rain when the weather turns. We have to make sure that they are kept warm in the worst days of cold. We give our word.

'Remember: the queen is the life of the hive. And you must listen to the bees. Once you get to know them, you will be able to tell their mood from the sound they make.'

We put our ears to one of the hives. A gentle murmur can be heard from within.

'But travelling with them is another story. The raft is in a sorry state. I'm not so sure if the bees would be safe on it. If a wave came ...'

'Maybe they could go on the balloon?' Helena says.

'But of course. Clever girl! We don't have any use for it and it has nothing but bad memories for everyone. We need to talk to Lili about it. See if she can get it airborne for you. If you handled a glider, you should be able to handle a balloon.'

'Plain sailing,' I say and we all laugh.

Lili starts working straight away, getting the balloon into working order again, explaining all the time to us how the wind has a mind of its own and the balloon only listens to it. How all I can do to control it is play with the gas, which allows it to fall or rise in an attempt to capture the winds that will move us forward.

She is good with these things and spreads the deflated bag on the ground, with the basket attached, checks the burner, then the valves, making sure that the fan is working to blow air into the bag.

'We will be sorry to see you go,' Irina says, watching Lili inflating the bag.

'If it wasn't for Father, we'd –'

'I understand.' She looks at her own daughter and puts her arms around her.

'But we'll return with him some day. Now that we've found you.'

It's a morning of light breezes, a good time to set off, because the wind isn't too strong. It was vicious winds that took us away; gentler breezes will sail us safely home. Everyone gathers at the harbour to see us off: bee-keepers, teachers, children, Helena.

The bag is half-inflated. Time to light the burner as Lili has shown me. Its flame shoots up into the sky. The air heats in the balloon and it slowly begins to take on its roundy shape, to rise, then some more until there is enough to pull the basket into its standing position. It's time for us to climb in. Esper stands up beside me, his arms around Veltor.

'And now the treasure that you came for.'

Irina and Helena stand before us laden down with boxes. The queen hands me another of Tartesah's books: The Way of the Bee.

'Everything you need to know about the little creatures is in there. It is where I learned all my knowledge. And here, her smoker, her decapping knife, hive tools. You know how to use them now. Take them with you and may they help you in your work.'

Then she hands us a big honeycomb and as many jars of honey as the basket can hold. 'The honey is for the bees only. Stores to keep them fed when there isn't enough nectar around.' Then she gently hands over a small box.

'This is the queen and her nurse bees, some drones. They will start your colony, so guard them with your life. It is up to you now to bring them back to Orchard Territory. Remember, they are more precious than all the gold in the world. If you treasure them, maybe in time your territory will be like this.'

'We hope it will,' Esper and I say in unison.

I keep adding fuel to the burner until it has enough for lift-off. Then, very gently, we start to move away from the ground.

'Goodbye, Irina. Goodbye, Helena. Goodbye, everyone. Thank you.'

'Come back to see us again,' they all cry.

'We promise.'

They wave and wave, their bodies getting smaller and smaller as we move up and over the charred remains of the hexagons, the bees' workplace, Tartesah's little house by the river where she once sat and wrote. We feel the heat from the burner, land slipping away and before we know it we are

UP

UP

UP

ACKNOWLEDGEMENTS

My deepest gratitude to:

Siobhán, Gráinne and all at Little Island for the great care and attention they have taken with every aspect of *Gold*.

Nuala Parkinson-Coombs, *Gold*'s first young reader, who helped me see the story from her perspective.

Peter, who walked the initial story with me up and down mountains, through flooded woods and across bogs as I plotted it out scene by scene.

Daniel, who didn't let me settle for the ordinary but pushed me to bring Starn and Esper on ever greater adventures.

Genevieve and Jake Hystad for the miracle of Lia.

Anne and Tony Duncan for giving me a key to that secret place in the woods of Moyamba, where I could sit with my two boys and let them tell their story. Such generosity!

My friends at Talking Stick, who listened faithfully to every chapter and kept me going week by week with their encouragement.

A special thank you to Máire Bradshaw of Bradshaw Books and Alan Hayes of Arlen House for getting me this far.

ABOUT THE AUTHOR

Geraldine Mills has been a poet and short-story writer for many years and has already published several books. This is her first novel, and her first book for children.

She lives with her husband in Oughteraard, outside Galway city, on the west coast of Ireland.

If you enjoyed *Gold*, you may also like
these titles from Little Island:

The Wordsmith by Patricia Forde
Valentina by Kevin McDermott
The Keeper by Darragh Martin
Good Red Herring by Susan Maxwell
Old Friends by Tom O'Neill

www.littleisland.ie